*The
Wedding
Party*

By Cara Connelly

Excerpt from *The Wedding Favor* copyright © 2013 by Lisa Connelly.
Excerpt from *The Wedding Dance* copyright © 2020 by Lisa Connelly.

Digital Edition MAY 2019 ISBN: 978-0-06-291075-2
Print Edition ISBN: 978-0-06-291076-9

Cover design by Nadine Badalaty
Cover photographs © Yuri_Arcurs/ iStock/Getty Images (couple);
ryoung/swedewah/iStock/Getty Images (Background)

Avon Impulse and the Avon Impulse logo are registered trademarks of HarperCollins Publishers in the United States of America.
Avon and HarperCollins are registered trademarks of HarperCollins Publishers in the United States of America and other countries.

FIRST EDITION

21 22 23   HDC   10 9 8 7 6 5 4 3 2 1

The Wedding Party

A SAVE THE DATE NOVELLA

CARA CONNELLY

AVONIMPULSE
An Imprint of HarperCollinsPublishers

For Billy

CHAPTER ONE

SOMEONE—MAKE THAT SOMEONE besides me—*really needs to take charge of this dress debacle.*

Turning her back on the bride's stubborn battle with an intractable zipper, Ellie Marone aimed a pleading look at the only other candidate for the job, her daughter Julie.

Julie's expression clearly said *Not it!*

Ellie sighed. Apparently, as Kate's matron of honor, it was up to her to deal out the tough love.

She stalled. Dealing out love to her best friend, that was easy. But being tough? Way harder. For four decades, she and Kate had faced the world arm-in-arm, dried each other's tears, fought each other's foes. Without Kate, well, Ellie didn't know how she would've survived Jake's death, much less pulled herself together to raise their two amazing daughters. It was no exaggeration to say that all of them, especially Ellie, owed Kate their lives.

And just three years ago when Ellie fell for the wrong guy and got her heart mangled again, Kate helped her through that too. And Ellie had gotten past it. Yes, she had.

Tomorrow Kate would finally marry the man of her dreams, and Ellie couldn't be happier for her. Sure, she worried that Kate might drift away from her. But she told herself that was rank paranoia. They were best friends for life, and Ellie would love Kate forever.

Unfortunately, Ellie now had to break the news to her that, at forty-eight, there was more of her to love than there used to be. The problem was, the task called for subtlety. Tact. Delicate euphemisms.

In other words, it called for anybody but Ellie.

At the high school where she'd once taught and now served as principal, Ellie's colleagues affectionately described her communication style as blunt, with a side of sarcasm. Sensitive understatement simply wasn't her strength.

But she owed it to Kate to be honest, and to herself to get it over with. Drawing a fortifying breath, she squared her shoulders and strode across the sunny bridal suite. "Kate," she said, looking her best friend in the eye, "if you want to get your size eight pooch into this size two dress, you're gonna have to suck it in."

"I'm sucking!" Kate gasped.

"We'll see about that." Stepping around behind her, Ellie got a grip on the tiny zipper tab and dragged it up, up, up as Kate pulled in her gut, hissed every atom of air from her lungs, and generally tried to make herself three sizes smaller than the good Lord had built her.

The zipper ground to a halt just north of Kate's waist. Lifting her gaze, Ellie met Kate's eyes in the full-length mirror. "Keep going," Kate gasped out.

It was futile, but Ellie put her back into it anyway, gaining another hard-fought inch before the zipper cried *Uncle*!

In the gap above it, Kate's flesh bunched and folded. "We've got back cleavage," Ellie informed her.

"Spread it out." A breathless whisper. "Use your fingers."

"For crying out loud, Kate, it's not butter."

But Ellie tried anyway, pressing and flattening and tucking. And still the zipper refused to budge. She threw up her hands. "It's not happening."

In the mirror, Kate shot her a death stare.

Without a word, Ellie turned her around and held up a hand mirror. For a long moment, Kate refused to look. When she did, she groaned weakly. The white satin wedding gown spread apart in a wide V.

"You can't," Ellie stated, "squeeze ten pounds of sausage into a five-pound sack."

"Mom!" Julie gasped.

"What? It's simple physics." She patted her wilting friend's shoulder. "Buck up, Kate. You're gorgeous and you know it. So what if you're not a size two like your great-granny was? Women were tiny back then. And they couldn't vote."

Kate frowned. "What does voting have to do with it?"

"Non sequitur alert," Julie chimed in. "Number four for the day, and it's only noontime. We could be looking at a new record, folks."

Ellie favored her with a smug smile. "The genius brain works in mysterious ways."

Julie pointed at Kate. "Thanks again for talking her into that stupid MENSA test."

"It wasn't so much talking as goading," Kate grumbled, letting the dress fall, "and I admit it backfired. I expected to outscore her by fifty points and have bragging rights forever. Who knew she was a closet genius?"

"She hid it well," Julie agreed.

Ellie waved a careless hand. "It's hardly surprising," she said loftily, "that your puny brains failed to recognize superior intellect."

"Oh please." Kate stomped to the closet, yanked a powder-blue sundress off a hanger and dragged it over her head, all while muttering about the difference between intelligence and common sense, who had which and who didn't, blah blah.

Ellie rose above it. Gathering up the wedding dress like a good matron of honor, she dumped it on the velvet chaise and dusted her hands. "Okay, that's out of the way. I don't know why you even bothered with that old thing when you've got a Givenchy waiting in the closet."

"Ginny Johnson, that's why," Kate admitted under her breath.

Ellie propped her fists on her hips. "You're *still* trying to impress that witch? High school was a long time ago, Kate. You need to make an appointment with yourself, lie down on that leather couch in your office, and analyze the hell out of why, as a successful psychiatrist with a Harvard degree on your wall, you haven't gotten over the fact that Ginny beat you out for prom queen *thirty years ago*."

Kate slumped pitifully. "She works it into the conversation every time I run into her."

"Uh-huh. And I bet the last time you saw her she made a crack about your wedding, about what a pity it is that it took you so long . . ." Inspiration struck, and Ellie snapped her fingers. "She told you she wore her granny's wedding dress, didn't she?"

Kate nodded glumly.

Silently, Ellie fumed. Nobody, but nobody, got to pick on Kate and walk away from it.

But she'd plot her revenge later. For now, "Big deal. So Skinny Ginny got her bony butt into her granny's dress sometime back in the last century. Since then, she's down two husbands and up forty pounds. Can't you see that she only lords it over you about the prom because she's *jealous* of everything you've accomplished since then?"

Kate perked up. "You really think so?"

"Yeah, I really think so," Ellie said, just as she said the last hundred times they'd had similar conversations. Apparently, wounds inflicted on young, innocent minds sank deep, and no matter how much time passed, a few simple words could start them bleeding again.

"As for your great-gran's dress," Ellie went on, "you would've fit into it back in 1995 too. But those days are gone, so pack it off to Goodwill and forget about it."

"Gee, Mom," Julie said, "don't get all sentimental on us."

"Sentiment won't get ten pounds of sausage—"

"Enough with the sausage!" Kate shoved her so she plopped down on the chaise. Ellie's butt landed on the wedding gown, her hand caught in the sleeve, and *riiiiip . . .*

"Oops." Ellie tried to seem contrite, but, "Sorry, Kate, that's on you—"

Kate pounced, flattening Ellie. "I'll give you sausage," she cried, gleefully smothering Ellie in handfuls of old satin.

Julie egged her on with a whoop. "Hold her down and I'll tickle her!"

"No!" Ellie shrieked. She was helpless against tickling, and when Julie's fingers found her ribs, she lost it completely. Trapped under ten yards of wedding dress and a hundred and thirty pounds of "sausage," she wriggled like a worm on a hook while Kate and Julie laughed like hyenas.

They might have kept it up for hours, but an über-masculine voice called out from the doorway. "Girl fight!"

Kate's fiancé, Mike Murphy, ambled into the room.

Which was totally awkward, seeing as how Ellie's wriggling had pushed her yellow sundress up around her waist.

But at least Mike's appearance put an end to the tickling, if not to the hysterics. Batting satin off her face, she saw Kate clutching her side. Julie was hiccupping.

Rising from the chaise with what dignity she could muster, Ellie quickly shimmied her dress down over her butt. Embarrassing, yes, but she couldn't really begrudge Mike a last glimpse of lace panties. At fifty, the man's legendary bachelorhood was coming to an end. From now on, the only panties he'd see were Kate's cotton high-rises.

Besides, it was worth any amount of humiliation to see Kate laughing again.

Speaking of Kate. Ellie finger-combed her chestnut hair back from her brow and pulled the pin on a grenade. "Sausage!"

Kate sprang at her. Ellie circled the chaise, sprinted for the door, dodged around Mike . . . and slammed into a solid wall of chest and abs.

Oh God, no! It can't be . . .

Tilting her head up, up, she found the face attached to all those muscles. Ryan Murphy—Ellie's three-years-ago heartbreak, and the last person in the world she wanted to chest bump.

She leapt back like he was lethal. Which he was, but not in the obvious way. Sure, he looked like the hardened SWAT-team veteran he was, with his close-cropped blond hair and steely blue eyes.

But all his guns didn't scare her, or his flash-bangs, or his black belt in karate. No, it was . . . everything else about him. His wacky humor, his huge heart. His shower-sex smile.

He should have a proximity warning tattooed on his armor-plated pecs:

STAY BACK OR I'LL SNEAK IN UNDER YOUR DEFENSES
AND KILL YOU WITH KINDNESS.
IF I DON'T SEX YOU TO DEATH FIRST.

She was in his crosshairs now. The surprise on his face was giving way to a grin. In a minute, he'd explode a testosterone bomb and she'd be caught in the fallout.

Backpedaling for dear life, she snagged her heel in the rug, teetered, would've fallen, but . . .

RYAN REACHED OUT and hauled Ellie in, pinning her to his chest with both arms. Total overkill for a minor stumble, but hell if he'd miss a chance at an armful of Ellie Marone. Any excuse would do.

Ellie wasn't having it, of course. She got her arms in between them and tried to pry her way out.

Not so fast, babe.

He held her for a few sweet seconds more, curling one palm around her delicate shoulder, sliding the other down to the familiar dip in the small of her back. Closing his eyes, he cradled her. Breathed her in, breathed her out.

And then, reluctantly, he let her go.

She stepped back, but her scent lingered in his nose. Her warmth imprinted his skin. He missed the feel of her already.

More accurately, after three long years, he missed the feel of her *still*.

Ellie obviously felt otherwise. On her face, shock had morphed into fury. "What the hell are *you* doing here?"

He lifted one brow, a talent she'd once adored. Now she ground her teeth. So he pushed it an extra half inch. "Best man," he said, biting back a grin when her green eyes widened in horror.

That's right, sweetheart, I'm here all weekend. You can't chase me away this time.

Mike clapped his shoulder, a wide grin on his face. "Ry got some time off work after all. When he turned up this morning, Kevin stepped aside so Ry could take over as best man."

Kate appeared beside her, squeezing Ellie's rigid arm. "That's terrific, Ry," she said, sounding sincere even with Ellie simmering beside her. "But I wish I'd known you were coming. Sunrise Bluff books solid for the Fourth. I'll ask the manager—"

"No worries," Ryan cut in. "I'll bunk with Mike."

Ellie's glare seared holes in him. Instead of meeting it, he glanced over her shoulder at the view out the bay window—rolling green lawn, sparkling blue sea.

"Nice place for a wedding," he said. A colossal understatement. Ogunquit, Maine, in July was a New England postcard, and the resort's location high on a bluff offered him a bird's-eye view of the shoreline: lobster boats trawling off the rocky coast to the south; sandy beach curving in a crescent to the north.

"My family's been coming here since the nineties," Kate said. "I always dreamed of getting married right out in that gazebo."

"And baby"—Mike engulfed her in his arms—"I'm here to make all your dreams come true."

Ellie faked a finger down her throat, which made Ryan chuckle. She always tried to pretend she wasn't sentimental, but he knew for a fact that she cried at commercials.

Now she narrowed her eyes at him, her stone-killer squint. Better than being ignored, but not as good as if she'd melted into his arms, sobbing that she couldn't live another day without him and begging him never to leave again.

Ruefully, he realized he'd been hoping for exactly that reaction. He should've known better. Giving him what he wanted had never been on Ellie's to-do list.

Instead, she marched to the sofa and vented her irritation on a pile of white satin, shaking it like a dog with a bone until it assumed the shape of a wedding dress.

Kate watched her with troubled eyes. "Ellie—"

Ellie spun around and aimed a finger at her. No words were exchanged, but Kate got the message. Wringing her hands, she turned to Julie. "So. How about some champagne?"

"I'm not so sure that's a good idea—" Julie began.

"It's brilliant," Ellie cut in. "I'll get it." She jammed the dress onto a hanger and rammed it into the closet, then stomped out of the sitting room. Ryan heard cupboards slamming in the kitchenette.

"That went well," he said to the room at large.

Kate offered a sympathetic smile. "I'm glad you're here, Ry. Totally glad. But"—with a *what the hell* look at Mike—"a heads-up would've been nice."

"Not Mike's fault," Ry cut in quickly. "Last-minute decision. I was supposed to be on call all month, but I managed to get some leave."

Not easy to do with the elevated threat level in LA, but after last week's disaster, his boss had declared that Ryan needed time off.

Maybe a lot of time.

But the upside was that he could be here when his brother married—*married!*—the woman who made him happier than even a lifetime of fast cars and faster women. Ryan was thrilled for him. He loved Kate too. So it was all good, right?

Wrong. Because apparently, he was still *in* love with Kate's best friend.

Which sucked large.

After putting all of America between them for the last three years and tucking half a dozen LA wannabe starlets under his belt, he'd been sure he was completely over Ellie. But one glimpse of her and he wanted to live inside her light again.

That's how he'd always felt, like the world was

brighter around Ellie. Like the sun shone stronger and everything was hotter.

Especially the sex. Forget the starlets. His chemistry with Ellie was scorching. Even now, with the kitchen door closed between them, he could feel her heat on his skin—

Someone punched his arm, hard. He peeled his gaze off the door and met Julie's narrowed green eyes.

Damn, she looked so much like—

"Don't," she growled, "tell me how much I look like Mom."

"But—"

"I mean it. You don't get to talk about her, not to me. You lost that right when you left Boston."

As if he'd had any choice. "She broke up with me, Jules. What was I supposed to do? Stick around and watch her with somebody else?"

Julie hard-eyed him. "You could've given her some time, Ry. She'd have come around."

"She'd have come around, all right. She'd have come around Mike's place with a new boyfriend." It would've torn his heart out, what was left of it after she'd broken it to pieces. "She made it crystal clear that she didn't want me. That I was nothing special."

"Baloney. She was crazy about you."

"Oh yeah?" His turn to be annoyed. "Then why did she throw my proposal back in my face?"

CHAPTER TWO

JULIE'S MOUTH FELL open. "You *proposed*? You actually asked Mom to marry you?"

"Yeah, I did," Ryan said, feeling the sting like it was yesterday. "She told me I was too young for her, and she laughed at me for even thinking about marriage. I figured the rest of you got a laugh out of it too."

"It's not funny, Ry. It's sad."

Even worse. "I don't need your pity—"

"Good, because you're not getting it. I'm sad for Mom."

"Wait, what?" That wasn't fair. "I'll say it again, Jules. *She* dumped *me*."

"She's allergic to commitment. You should know that about her."

"Knowing it and curing her of it are two different things." He'd tried. He'd even thought he succeeded.

They were magic together. How could she not want that magic for the rest of their lives?

He looked away from Julie's green eyes, so much like Ellie's. How the hell was he gonna get through this weekend? He should've stayed in LA, or headed to Cabo—

Ellie bustled out of the kitchen, tray of glasses in one hand, bottle of Moët in the other. Bending over to set everything on the coffee table, she gave him an excellent view of her excellent ass.

"God, she looks great," he murmured. "Better than ever."

"Better than ten minutes ago, for sure. Her cheeks are pinker. Her eyes are shooting sparks."

"It's her pissed-off face." He knew it well.

Ellie twisted the cork and it exploded from the bottle. Champagne foamed out, spilling over her fingers. "Shit," she sputtered, giving her hand a quick shake.

Then she proceeded to suck her fingers. Ry's lungs collapsed, releasing a silent groan. She didn't even know how sexy she was.

Longing must have been written on his face, because Julie sounded almost sympathetic. "Listen, Ry, I'm probably violating some kind of sacred mother/daughter code here, but you need to know—she ate her heart out after you left."

He wanted to believe it, but . . . "Not possible. She said—"

"Forget what she said three years ago. Think about

her reaction right now, today. You said it yourself, she's pissed off, right? But we both know she doesn't get pissed at her exes. She just"—Julie fluttered her fingers—"lets them go."

That was true. He'd seen it happen to other poor schmucks before he got involved with her.

"But you, Ryan Murphy," Julie added with another arm punch for emphasis, "she never let go of."

ELLIE LET A long, icy swallow of champagne slide down her throat.

Then another.

She wasn't usually a chugger, but as of five minutes ago she'd decided the weekend would look a lot better through the bottom of a wineglass.

Kate came up beside her. "Thanks for that moving toast," she said dryly, snatching the bottle from Ellie's hand.

"Oh please. You'll get plenty of fanfare this weekend without me fawning over you."

"I knew I should've asked Carol to be my matron of honor."

"It's not too late. I can pack in ten minutes, be back in Boston for supper."

"You wish. And it wouldn't matter anyway. He'd be right behind you."

"Who?"

Kate snorted. "You're the genius. Figure it out." She filled two flutes and went off to play slap and tickle with Mike.

Ellie glugged another long swallow.

"Mom," Julie called from across the room. She mimed a drinking motion with one hand.

Ellie made a *Do I have to wait on everybody* face back at her.

Julie gave her an exaggerated *Yeah you do* nod.

Caving in to the inevitable, Ellie poured two more glasses, reluctantly abandoned her own glass on the coffee table, and strode smartly toward her daughter, pretending to ignore the two hundred pounds of heartache standing alongside her.

Julie snatched a glass with a snide, "It's about time."

"I'm so sorry," Ellie sweetly replied. "I didn't realize your legs were broken or I would've rushed right over."

Ryan accepted his with a much more gracious, "Thanks, Ellie."

She spared him a cool nod, but the deep, familiar rumble of his voice triggered a fevered response all the way to her core.

She turned away, meaning to douse it but good with another frosty slug of champagne, but Julie caught her hand and held on to it. "I was just about to fill Ry in on the schedule of events," she said.

"There's a schedule?" That deep rumble again, with a startled lilt at the end.

"I'll email it to you," Julie said. "But here's the quick

and dirty. Seven-thirty dinner tonight at Magnolia's for the wedding party—"

He held up a large calloused hand. "Who else is in the wedding party?"

"Well, there's Mike and Kate, of course. And you and Mom."

"Just the four of us?"

Ellie made the mistake of meeting his eyes. Lord, they were blue. And they were all over her.

Well, actually they were staring deeply into hers, but it felt like he was taking her in all at once, absorbing every part of her and stripping her naked while he was at it. She was hyperaware of him too, from chiseled jaw to the hard body she knew as intimately as her own, now hiding under a faded T-shirt and jeans.

She unlocked eyes with him. "About dinner," she said to Julie. "I told Kate that you and Cody want to come."

Julie's eyes popped. "I never said that."

"You didn't have to. I knew you felt left out. Your sister too. So I took care of it." She patted Julie's arm. "I always take care of my girls."

And with that, she slipped her hand free from her daughter's and beat a—sedate, measured—retreat across the room to her glass.

Behind her, she heard Julie complaining to Ryan. "There go the only two waking hours of the weekend I would've had alone with my husband. Thanks a lot for that."

"Me?" Ry said in that mesmerizing voice.

"She doesn't want to be alone with you," Julie informed him.

That was the God's honest truth. Ellie shuddered at the thought. Kate and Mike would be all over each other, leaving her to make conversation with Ry. What if he told her he was seeing someone? In love? Engaged!

She took a pull on her flute. She'd be glad for him, of course. He was young, healthy, virile . . .

She fanned herself, threw an accusing glance at the air-conditioning vent.

Anyway, yeah, he was all that, so she'd definitely be happy for him if he'd finally found a girl his age— meaning someone at least nine years younger than herself. That's what he needed, not a cougar like her.

Fun and games, well, that was one thing. She and Ry had had plenty of those. But that was before he'd lost his mind and proposed, spouting nonsense about love and destiny.

Honestly. They'd been good together, sure. Deliciously good.

But Destined To Be Together? No way. She'd given Destiny a try thirty years ago, and that bitch had ripped her heart out and run it through a meat grinder, then shoved it back in her chest and expected her to get on with her life.

She'd done her best. Survived. Even managed to enjoy it.

But a wound like that never healed. You just learned

to live with the pain.

So no, she wouldn't be giving Destiny another chance to gut her. That was the whole reason she made a point of dating younger men, so she wouldn't get serious about them. So that even if someone like Ry came along to tempt her, vanity would keep her from giving in to temptation. Because really, who wanted to grow old ten years before her husband? To sag, and wrinkle up, and watch her hair go thin while he was still strong and vital and handsome?

Not Ellie Marone. She'd make that long, slow decline on her own, thank you very much. And when she died, she wouldn't leave behind a husband to face the world alone.

Or worse yet, to face it with a twenty-four-year-old blonde on his arm—

A finger tapped her shoulder. "What time should I pick you up?" Ry said from about two inches behind her.

She giant-stepped forward before turning to answer him. "I don't need a ride."

He smiled, putting a dimple in his left cheek.

She loved that dimple.

"Then you can drive me," he said.

"Nobody's driving anybody. The restaurant's two blocks from here."

"So we can walk over together."

"I don't want to walk with you."

"Why not?"

"Your legs are too long. And you think everything's

a race."

His smile widened. She noticed his front tooth was chipped. How did that happen? She set her jaw, refusing to ask.

"I promise to walk as slow as you want."

"You always say that, then you lope along like a cheetah."

"Maybe I've changed."

She looked him up and down. At thirty-nine, he was all hard muscle on the outside, hard-won confidence on the inside. His stance, his expression, everything about him spelled "powerful" with a capital P.

"Well, you're scrawnier," she deadpanned, "but I doubt that'll slow you down."

He crossed his arms, so his biceps stood out like grapefruit. Allowed her a minute to absorb their awesomeness. "I could walk backward."

Great. Instead of watching his butt pull ahead of her, she'd see his face the whole time.

Face. Arms. Butt. She didn't want to see any of it!

She hardened her resolve. "Walk on your hands, for all I care. But you're not walking with me."

CHAPTER THREE

RYAN DROPPED INTO the chair across the table from Ellie. "How the hell?" he asked her. He'd kept an eye on her door for the last hour and never seen her slip out.

She gave him an innocent look.

Yeah, right.

He signaled the waitress, ordered Dewar's on the rocks.

"Another cabernet for me," Ellie added.

He eyed her. Rosy cheeks, a permanent half smile. She probably thought getting drunk would make it easier to deal with him.

No such luck, Ellie. He'd damned well be in her face all night, doing his best to make her regret pushing him out of her life.

He lifted an eyebrow at her. "So the wrong number

from the front desk, that was your doing?" The call had drawn him away from the window for a crucial thirty seconds. "Clever."

A smug smile. "Haven't you heard? I'm a genius."

"A genius who has the desk clerk in thrall."

"You make me sound like a vampire."

He glanced meaningfully at her glass. She raised it, swirling the bloodred wine, then drank down a swallow.

He laughed. So did she, a lovely, intimate sound.

And just like that, three lonely, shitty years fell away as if they'd never happened. As if he and Ellie had never been apart. Happiness flooded through him. Bantering with Ellie, watching her eyes light up when she got off a good one, was better than having sex with anyone else. Her laughter was music, his favorite sappy song.

Back in his room, he'd vowed to himself that he'd get through the weekend without letting her see how deep his hurt ran, and his love. That he'd play it cool, keep it light, keep it fun. That he'd get himself back to LA in one piece, back on the job by next week.

But now, gazing into her smiling eyes, her beloved face, he knew that nothing else in the world would ever look as beautiful to him. Not the coastline at Big Sur, not the sunset off Malibu. He could stare at her forever and never get tired of the view.

Forgetting all the promises he'd made to himself, he

spoke from his heart without stopping to check in with his head.

"God, Ellie, you're gorgeous."

FOR A LONG moment Ellie held Ry's gaze, bluer than the sea, before she managed to break the connection.

And that right there was the downside of wine—it lowered her resistance to a nice pair of eyes. Not to mention a crooked smile, long muscular arms, and large tanned hands with magic fingers, five of which were splayed on the pristine white tablecloth.

She dragged her eyes away from those fingers too. They were every bit as dangerous as his eyes, immutably associated as they were with the best sex of her life.

She needed help here, a distraction, because things were getting way too intimate. His words had gone straight to her heart—and straight to the heart of her fears. Sure, she looked good *now*, but in a few years . . .

Ry moved his hand like he might reach for hers. Casually, she leaned back and dropped her own hands to her lap.

Where were her daughters when she needed them?

She shot a glance over at Kate and Mike. Their foreheads were touching, their fingers entwined. No help there.

"Ellie—"

"You look good too, Ry," she said matter-of-factly,

cutting him off before he could say something else that would make her heart leap and ache all at once. "LA must agree with you. All that sand and surf."

"It's okay." His gaze fell, and she felt disconcertingly like the sun had set, leaving her in twilight.

"Take up surfing yet?" she asked, then wanted to bite her tongue. It was too personal. He'd know she remembered their plans for a week at surf camp in Mexico, a trip that never happened thanks to his stupid proposal.

Sure enough, he lifted his eyes again. The sun came out from behind a cloud.

"Actually no," he said after a telling pause. "I guess I felt—"

"Too bad," she cut in again, keeping her tone light, "you'd love it. I do." She hated to get nasty, but damn it, he was pushing her into it.

"So you learned to surf without me?" The hurt in his voice was a knife in her gut.

But there was anger in his tone too, and that was a good thing, because if he got mad enough he'd stop looking at her like he wanted to eat her up, or kiss her, or throw her down on the table and tear her clothes off.

Sipping her wine, she eyed him innocently over the lip. "Of course I did. Not at a camp. In Hawaii."

He nodded slowly. His posture hadn't changed but his shoulders had tensed. "Let me guess. You met up with some international surfing phenomenon and he offered you private lessons."

She huffed a short laugh. "Not exactly. I mean, he's big at the *national* level—"

He leaned forward suddenly, rocking the table. "Goddamn it, Ellie, you never gave a rat's ass about surfing. I had to talk you into that camp."

She widened her eyes. "So I was supposed to drop every activity we ever did together?"

"Yes!" His raised voice drew a startled glance from the waitress, who set their drinks down and fled.

Ellie leaned forward too, anger driving her voice down instead of up. "Does that mean you haven't had sex since you left? No California girls heating up your sheets?"

He sat back, lips taut. "Don't even, Ellie."

"No, don't *you* even, Ry. We broke up three years ago. *Three years.* I haven't been sitting around in a chastity belt, and neither have you."

"Did you even wait till I left Boston? Did you even *care* that I left?"

Her turn to sit back. "I didn't ask you to leave."

"You didn't ask me to stay."

She threw up her hands. "I didn't ask you to come to this wedding either! Why are you here anyway? I thought you were indispensable to the LAPD."

He snorted. "Who told you that?"

"Your brother, who else? He brags about you constantly. The hero in the family."

The anger leached from Ry's eyes. His whole face seemed to shut down.

"What's wrong?" she asked, more worried now than mad. "Did something happen?"

He crossed his arms over his chest. "Why would you think that?"

"Why are you answering every question with a question?"

He looked away, past her shoulder. Nothing to see there but a blank wall, yet he stared hard at it as seconds ticked by.

Ellie waited. And waited.

She'd been down this road before. Ry was better than most men at airing his feelings, but there were things he was even better at, things like taking on blame he didn't deserve, shouldering guilt he had no business bearing, and generally feeling responsible for every screw-up no matter who made it. And in a job like his, screw-ups could have fatal consequences.

It was those things he was always reluctant to share. But if she waited long enough, gave him her silent attention while his brain circled around and around like a dog before it settled, he'd eventually come out with it.

In bits and pieces, he'd come out with it.

His arms uncrossed at last. He reached for his scotch but left it on the table, rotating the glass, making damp rings on the tablecloth. She waited, tuned into him, oblivious to everything else around them.

A long moment passed before he raised his head. Maybe ready to give her that first bit or piece.

Instead he said, "So where is he? Your surfer. When's

he getting here?" When she didn't reply, he raised mocking brows. "What, you ditched him already? No date for the wedding?"

Pushing her glass away and folding her hands, Ellie assessed him coolly. Despite the pain in his eyes, she recognized the challenge in his tone. He was baiting her. Distracting her and salving his wounded ego at the same time. Looking for leverage to start a fight.

Well, she wasn't born yesterday, not by a mile. She knew exactly how to deal with Ryan Murphy.

Curving her lips in a half smile, she said ruefully, "I would've brought the supermodel I'm currently sleeping with, but she had a photo shoot this weekend."

CHAPTER FOUR

RELIEF COURSED THROUGH Ry. For a minute there she'd thrown him off with the supermodel crack, but if there was one immutable truth he knew about Ellie, it was how she liked her sex—hot, hard, and hetero all the way.

So why try to persuade him otherwise? What was she trying to hide?

Could Julie be right? Did Ellie still want him? Was she afraid she'd give in to her feelings if he pushed her?

That would explain a few things. Like how pissed off she was to see him here. The cruel way she'd thrown the surfer in his face. Her feeble attempt to make him believe she'd switched teams.

He couldn't help grinning, which made her eyes narrow, which only made him grin wider. Ellie thought she was so clever, but he was onto her. If nothing else, she'd given the game away when he'd stupidly let on that something had gone wrong in LA. Worry had furrowed her brow.

She still cared about him.

Now he had two days to make her admit it. Two days to remind her how good they were together, to convince her to quit pushing him away. Two days to get back into her bed, and into her heart.

It wouldn't be easy, but when had Ellie ever been easy?

She must have seen the resolve settle over him, because she got a mulish look on her face. "Ryan," she began, then clammed up when Julie pulled out the chair next to her.

"Sorry we're late," Julie said. "Cody needed to chill for a few after making that drive."

Trying not to resent the intrusion, Ry rose and stuck out a hand to the big guy helping Julie into her seat. "You must be Cody. I'm Ryan." They shook, and Ry flagged down the waitress. "What're you drinking?" he asked Cody.

"Something long and cold," Cody said, his Texas drawl widening the waitress's pretty brown eyes. "Whatever's on tap'll do. And bring my wife here a nice smooth cabernet."

Thanks to Ellie's last-minute additions, their rectangular table for eight was crammed into an alcove sized for a four-top. Cody took an end seat, close enough to Julie that he easily reached her thigh under the table.

Ry recognized the move, and a sharp stab of envy prompted him to rub knees with Ellie. She moved hers aside. He followed. She glared at him. "Quit manspreading," she said.

He smirked, feeling better about things, and offered Cody a friendly smile. "How long were you on the road?"

"Four hours." Cody relaxed back in his chair, releasing an end-of-the-work-week sigh. "Your Boston traffic's a hot bitch."

"Every Friday in July," Ry agreed.

"Ry lives in LA now," Kate said, emerging from her cocoon with Mike to make nice with the guests. "Talk about traffic. But you probably travel by chopper, don't you, Ry? Dropping down into the middle of a hostage crisis or whatever?"

He felt Ellie watching him. So perceptive, his Ellie.

He kept his smile in place. "Not every day, Kate. Mostly I sit in traffic like everyone else."

Before she could follow up, he said to Cody, "I hear you rode the circuit." Nothing could impress Ry more. Sure, Cody was a doctor now, head of the ER at Boston's busiest hospital. But rodeo riders, they were the toughest of the tough.

"Long time ago," Cody said, accepting his beer from the waitress with a smile that nearly undid her.

Ellie aimed a finger at him. "Holster that smile, young man, before you start a riot."

Ryan's lips twitched in annoyance. *Young man*, she

called Cody, even though he had to be at least thirty-five—just a few years younger than Ry.

If she meant to remind him that he was as close to Julie's age as to Ellie's, he could have told her that he'd heard it all before, on the day he proposed. Because it had seemed so important to her, he'd tried arguing about it, pointing out that Ellie had gotten married at seventeen and had Julie six months later. Hell, he knew sisters who were farther apart in age than that.

But the fact was, for him, age was beside the point. He wanted to be with Ellie for the rest of their lives, no matter how long or short.

The subtext was lost on Julie, who was all about her husband. "Cody's got one of those buckles," she told Ry, "the kind rodeo guys get for winning stuff. And he's got this sick scar on his ass too."

Cody grinned and ran his knuckles down his wife's bare arm. "Jules is way more impressed by the scar than the buckle."

"Well, the buckle's big," she said, "but the scar's even bigger."

Damn, the guy made Ry feel like a wimp, which wasn't easy to do. "How'd you get it? The scar, I mean. Was it a bull?"

"It was a fence," Cody said flatly.

Okaaaay, that could still be cool. "So, like, in a competition?"

"In my backyard." Cody must've seen his face fall,

because he let out a laugh. "Sorry to disappoint you, man. I got tossed off a horse I had no business being up on, and I busted through a fence ass first. A splinter as big as your arm damn near ripped my nuts off."

Ryan's own nuts curled up in tight little balls. "Still," he said staunchly. The guy was a legit cowboy. What could be cooler than that?

"Ryan heads up a SWAT team," Ellie piped in. "He puts his nuts on the line every day."

Huh?

"Remember a few years ago," she went on, "when that crazy guy shot up a Store 24 in Boston? Took a woman and her four-year-old hostage?" She gestured at Ryan with her wineglass. "Ry led the team that brought him down. Threw himself in front of the kid, took three rounds in his bulletproof vest. You must've seen him on TV. It was national news."

Cody's brows went up. "That was you? Damn, you've got nerves of steel, brother."

Ry shot Ellie a look. At the time, she hadn't seemed too impressed by what she'd termed his "heroics." In fact, it was just a week later that she'd flatly rejected his proposal, kicking him to the curb in the process.

So why now, of all times, did she suddenly decide to play whose balls are bigger? Now, when his nerves were more spaghetti than steel.

"Just another day in the life," Mike chimed in. "Even when we were kids, Ry was the guy who made the bullies back down." A proud grin for baby brother. "Dude was born to be a cop. And not just any cop. The first one through the door—"

"Wearing head-to-toe body armor," Ry pointed out firmly before Mike got carried away, "and armed to the teeth. It's nothing like bull riding," he added, passing the buck back to Cody. "You guys go into the ring in nothing but Wranglers. That takes *real* guts."

"What it takes," Cody drawled with a smile, "is a real lack of brains."

"Did someone say brains?" Amelia said, plopping down in the seat beside Ryan. "Is Mom bragging about MENSA again?" She accepted his kiss on the cheek. "It's great to see you, Ry," she said quietly.

"You too." Emotion roughened his voice. Rising, he caught her husband, Ray, in a bro-hug. He'd once assumed they'd all be family. He missed them every day.

When he sat down again, Amelia elbow-bumped him. "So, did Mom tell you she's a genius?"

"She might've mentioned it."

"Worked it into the conversation, did she?" Amelia rolled her eyes at Ellie's faux-innocent smile. "Tell him your IQ score, Mom, and get it over with."

"I really shouldn't," Ellie said. "I know how inferior it makes the rest of you feel."

"Pfft." That came from Kate. "She wants you to beg, Ry, so she can drag out the conversation as long as possible."

He cocked his head. "Okay, I'll bite. Ellie, what was your score?"

"Let's just say it was higher than hers." She tipped her chin at Kate.

"I had a bad day," Kate grumbled.

Ellie snickered.

"It was 132," Amelia said dryly. "She barely made the cut."

"You see why I don't talk about it?" Ellie said. "All the non-geniuses get so touchy."

"You don't know that we're not geniuses," Julie said. "We haven't been tested."

"Way to keep hope alive, dear." Ellie patted her hand.

Ray leaned around behind Amelia. "Ignore them, Ry, or they'll keep it up all night."

Ry was actually enjoying it, perfectly content to be in the midst of the Marone women again, every one of them a looker, every one a pisser. But the other men's expressions said they'd heard all this genius stuff before.

They didn't know how lucky they were.

"Big bonfire at our place," Ray went on. "You in?"

"Tonight?" It wasn't on the schedule Julie had sent him.

Amelia tore herself away from the ongoing argument. "We're renting a house on Wells Beach," she told him, "and lo and behold, there's a fire pit on the beach. Champagne, moonlight, romance—"

"And s'mores," Ellie added, rubbing her hands.

Julie snorted. "Real romantic, Mom."

"They can be," Ry said.

Ellie quit rubbing her hands and shot him a look. When he returned a slow smile, her cheeks turned pink.

No doubt she was recalling, as he was, their first and only camping trip to the White Mountains. She'd lasted one night before a cloudburst that coincided with her three a.m. nature call had her dialing up the nearest hotel.

Before that, though, they'd shared an idyllic evening. Cuddling by the campfire, roasting hot dogs on sticks, and finding new and interesting ways to enjoy s'mores.

Now he walked his gaze down the slender column of her throat, then lower, lingering on the swell of her breasts where they peeked out of her top. His tongue touched his lips. He could almost taste the sweet/salty flavor of melted chocolate and marshmallow licked off her—

She set her wineglass down with a thump. "On second thought," she snapped, "I'll skip the s'mores."

CHAPTER FIVE

RAY AND AMELIA'S rental was a sprawling old beach house, built a hundred years ago and never updated since. Some might call it dilapidated, but Ryan thought it was beautiful, its cedar shakes faded to grey by the salty sea air, the deck boards scoured smooth by decades of blowing sand.

What it lacked in amenities, it more than made up for in location, standing with its toes in the dunes. By the time he arrived with Mike and Kate, a bonfire blazed on the beach. Ray and Cody fed it driftwood while Amelia and Julie spread blankets on the sand.

There was no sign of Ellie on the beach, so Ry let the lovebirds drift toward the fire while he circled back to the kitchen. He found her pouring a bag of ice into a cooler.

His footsteps were lost in the racket, so when he said,

"Need some help?" she shot up straight, spraying ice cubes across the floor. The menacing look that followed had him scooping them up double-time.

She pointed at the sink.

"Five-second rule," he said.

"Have you seen this floor?"

He peered at it and, yeah, he dumped the cubes in the sink.

"While you're at it," she added, "quit sneaking up on me. This house is creepy enough."

He glanced around. Run-down for sure, but, "Creepy?"

She started pulling beers out of the old avocado-green refrigerator, passed them over, and he wiggled them into the ice. "Some guy offed his wife here a few years ago," she said, "then shot himself. In there." She aimed a thumb at the pantry. "Since then, people have seen some things."

"What kind of things?"

"Creepy things." She passed him a bottle of Prosecco, another of chardonnay. "Things like lights on when nobody's here."

"Timers."

"Shadows moving around inside."

"Prowlers."

She eye-rolled impatiently. "People aren't dumb, Ry. Prowlers would leave some evidence."

"So it's ghosts?"

"You said it, I didn't."

"But you were thinking it."

"You don't know what I was thinking."

"Because you're a genius and I'm just a dumb cop?"

She slapped the fridge shut. "Quit putting words in my mouth. And quit looking at me like that."

"Like what?"

"Like . . ." She churned a hand in the air.

"Like I want to back you up? Lock your wrists over your head? Kiss you?" As he spoke he moved steadily closer, until her back was pressed to the fridge, with just a hand's-breadth of air left between them.

She swallowed, and his gaze followed the movement of her throat, so sensual, so female. His caveman stirred, shoving civilized Ry aside.

Bracing both hands on the fridge on either side of her head, he caged her without touching her. His intentions were surely spelled out on his face, because she sucked a quick breath—arousal, but apprehension too. She was afraid. Not of him, he was sure, but of the two of them alone in this room where anything could happen. Where something was about to.

Subtle tremors ran through her, too slight for the naked eye, but his senses were wide open and his primal instincts responded, commanding him to cuff her wrists, take her mouth. Take her body.

Faintly, from the front of his brain, twenty-first-century Ryan called out. *Too soon, brother. Give her some time.*

But the heat. It poured from her skin, feeding his

own fire, the flames burning up his blood and his bones. He raked her with his gaze, from trembling knees to heaving breasts. Surely she wanted this too . . .

But when he dragged his gaze up from her chest to her eyes, he saw a different kind of heat there—hot defiance.

Apparently civilized-Ry was right. She wasn't ready to go caveman with him.

Yet.

He summoned his willpower. It was slow to respond.

But eventually, twenty-first-century Ryan took control. Ellie must've sensed him pull back from the edge, because the anger slowly faded from her eyes. Predictably, the defiance remained.

"Back off," she said, just a hint of tremolo betraying her arousal. She wanted him too. She was just too stubborn to admit it.

Yet.

"It's your call," he said. "Always has been. Always will be."

Gazing down into her deep green eyes, he watched her defiance melt away. Slowly, giving her all the time in the world to object, he moved his hands to her shoulders, slid his palms lightly down velvet skin to her elbows, then up again, mesmerized by the feel of her.

Her chest rose and fell rapidly, drawing his gaze again. Her black tank top clung to her curves. Showed off perfect breasts.

"They're not perfect," she said sharply, clueing him

in that he'd spoken aloud. "They're not pert. They're not even the same size."

"I remember," he murmured. His right hand slid three inches to the left, cupped a breast. "I like this one best." His other hand slid to the right. "Except for this one."

"Ryan." Her voice had gone breathy. "This isn't a good—"

He captured her lips with his, trapping her words. They were only that, words. But this, this was feeling. Sensation. It shivered over his skin. Ran wild through his veins.

He deepened the kiss, making damn sure she felt it too. And when she quivered, when her knees went soft, satisfaction lit him up . . . and inspiration struck.

He already knew what he wanted—her heart, all of it, completely and forever.

And now he knew how to get it.

It wouldn't be easy. She had defenses, Ellie did. She'd been fortifying them for years. She probably had a gun turret with his name on it.

But all of those walls barricaded her *heart*. Her body she'd left largely undefended. And not to sound conceited, but he had good reason to believe that body was particularly vulnerable to him.

Which meant that the best way, the only way, to Ellie's heart was through her panties.

It would be a battle. He'd need all the weapons he had—hands, lips, cock, dirty mouth—to breach the satin and lace. But once he was inside, he wouldn't stop until he took her over entirely.

First her body, then her heart.

She'd resist, of course. Once she realized that he'd snuck in through the back door, her mind—that genius brain he adored—would pull out every lame argument, every silly cliché.

But that was a struggle for another day. For now he had to convince her that all he wanted from her was a hit-and-run weekend of hot sex.

Sliding one hand up, he pushed his fingers into her hair. Used the other to cradle her cheek, gently angling her head, dragging his mouth slowly down, over her jaw, along the silky length of her neck.

Her pulse tripped madly under his tongue. A moan slid from her throat. Her arms came up, palms skimming his back, tugging him closer—

"Hey, Mom." Julie barreled through the screen door. "Everyone's waiting for the—oh shit, oh no. Sorry!"

Retreating footsteps. The screen door slapped shut. And the sensual spell he'd woven shattered like glass.

Stiffening, Ellie gave his shoulders a shove. "Get off me, you big lunkhead."

RYAN STEPPED BACK, but his eyes didn't release her. Dark with passion, they pinned Ellie to the fridge just as surely as his hips had done a moment before.

The difference was that his body heat was gone, and

she missed it. Which pissed her off. How could she have let him get his hands on her? Any woman with half a brain would know that making out with Ry was just one short step away from screwing him on the kitchen floor.

Estrogen responded to testosterone, and Ry was made of the stuff.

He dragged the back of one tanned hand across his mouth. Desire burned in his eyes, scorching her from two feet away.

"Don't try to tell me you don't want me," he said hoarsely.

Oh boy did she want him. He must see it in her burning cheeks, her heaving chest.

"I don't want you," she said anyway.

"Liar."

"Egomaniac."

A long moment passed as he watched her, searing her skin with blue flame.

"It can be just sex," he said finally. "I might be an egomaniac, but I know how to fuck you. I know how you like it."

Her bare toes curled. Sex with Ry would be so, so good.

And such a bad idea.

He peeled his sweatshirt over his head, held it out to her. A half smile curved his lips. "You look cold," he said, dropping his gaze to her chest.

She glanced down. Her nipples poked hard at her shirt.

Snatching the sweatshirt, she said stiffly, "The beach gets chilly at night."

As she dragged it over her head, she inhaled through her nose, a long, deep sniff of his familiar scent. Part soap, all man.

But when her head popped out through the neck, she gave him the glare he deserved. "Carry the cooler out, will ya? I've got things to do."

She would have turned her back on him, but he closed the distance between them by half, close enough to touch her, though he kept his hands to himself. He used his deep voice to lure her instead. "Just sex, Ellie. Sweaty. Nasty. All night long."

She swallowed hard. Pushed the words out through dry lips. "You know I don't do that."

"Don't have sweaty, nasty, all-night sex?" That half smile again. "Liar."

"That's not what I meant. I don't have sex unless I'm in a relationship." She tried to put annoyance into it. Failed. Her heart was beating too hard.

He spread his hands. "We're friends, right? That's a relationship. Friends with benefits."

So tempting. She wet her lips. He saw. Wet his own.

Stepping even closer, he dropped his voice, low and seductive. "Just for the weekend, Ellie." His hand came up, knuckles grazing her breast. Her nipple tightened to an impossible peak, the heavy sweatshirt no defense against the thrill of his touch.

Slowly, his knuckles skated up along her neck, her jaw. She fought the instinct to rub against them like a cat.

He opened his hand, cupped her cheek. Traced her ear with his fingertips. She tried to stay strong, but he must feel her trembling.

Curling his palm around her neck, he settled it there, thumb lightly stroking her pulse. "Just fun and games, the way you like it." His words whispered over her skin. "*Every* way you like it."

A long moment passed, both of them motionless except for the soft slide of his thumb.

Then he stepped back, fingertips trailing across her cheek until he let his hand fall. Breaking their gaze at last, he hefted the cooler onto one muscled shoulder and headed for the door.

On the threshold he paused briefly, cast her a last smoldering glance. "Think about it, babe."

As if she'd be able to think about anything else.

CHAPTER SIX

Ry plunked the cooler down on the sand beside Julie.

"Sorry," she said meekly.

He shrugged. "The night's young."

"True. It's only ten o'clock and you already made it to second base."

"Creepy, Jules."

"Believe me, I wish I could unsee it." Opening the cooler, she dug out two Coronas. "Grab some sand."

He hesitated. He wasn't really in the mood to talk to anyone but Ellie. But Kate's brothers had shown up, along with their wives and teenagers. He didn't know them well, but he didn't want to be rude. So he took the bottle Julie offered and sat down cross-legged, exchanging a few words as they each stopped by the cooler for beer.

"About the breakfast cruise," Julie said when they got a minute alone.

"Yeah, about that," he said. "I was thinking—"

"Forget it," she cut in. "If I have to get up at the ass crack of dawn, so do you."

"Wait, *dawn*? No." He was already shaking his head. His fatigue was bone-deep, part jetlag, part recovery from the bitch of a head whack that had earned him this "vacation."

"Okay, it's not dawn exactly. But nine o'clock, which is pretty damn early after a midnight bonfire, am I right?"

"Yeah, I might sleep through that one—"

"Only if you want Kate storming your room and bouncing on the end of your bed."

It wasn't Kate he wanted bouncing on his bed . . . But that was a different subject entirely.

"I get the picture," he said. "So . . . nine a.m. cruise—"

"Out of Perkins Cove, so set your wakeup call for eight."

"You realize that's five a.m. California time? Which actually is the ass crack of dawn."

"Blame it on the bride and groom. Anyway, we'll be back by noon. Plenty of time for a nap before the wedding at four."

"A nap sounds good." A nap with Ellie. They used to nap a lot after wearing each other out with Saturday-morning sex. And Saturday-afternoon sex. Yeah, they'd sexed and slept away many a Saturday . . .

"Ick," Julie said, eyeing his grin.

Cody lowered his lanky form onto the sand beside her. "What're you icking about?"

"Ryan's thinking perverted thoughts. About my mother."

"I thought you were good with that," Cody said, taking the beer she handed to him.

"Sure," she hissed impatiently, "but I don't want to read the details on his face."

Draping one arm across her shoulders, Cody reached around her and tapped his bottle to Ry's. "You can't win, man."

"Don't I know it," Ry replied sincerely.

Cody tried to do him a favor by changing the subject. "So, LA. What's that like?"

Ry's gut tightened, along with every other muscle in his body. Thanks to the clusterfuck that went down before he left, his job was the last thing he wanted to talk about.

So he talked all around it; the beach, the mountains, saying a lot of nothing until fate intervened in the form of Ray slamming his finger in the car door. Amelia dragged him over to Cody for a doctor's opinion—"Bruised but not broken"—and Ry used the commotion to slip away.

Stepping outside the ring of firelight, he circled around to the dunes where he found a massive tree trunk that some monster storm had long ago flung up on the beach and the tide had since polished like marble. He settled back against it and braced his forearms on bent knees. The half-empty bottle dangled from his fingers.

Closing his eyes, he drew a slow, deep breath. The

waves rolled in to shore, breaking with a soft hiss. Gradually, their steady rhythm slowed his racing pulse, smoothed his jagged thoughts.

Sipping his beer, he half listened to the conversations circulating around the bonfire, the familiar cadence of Boston accents punctuated by a lone Texas twang.

The other half of his mind was on Ellie, waiting for her footsteps. He could almost feel her fingertips brushing his cheek, her palm resting lightly on his shoulder for balance as she kicked off her sandals and sank onto the sand beside him.

But that was just a memory, a throwback to lazy weekends on the Cape, lolling on the beach all day, rolling in the sheets all night. Back then she'd touched him constantly. They couldn't keep their hands off each other.

Now he pressed his empty palm to the cool sand. Scooped it up and let it run through his fingers like time. Lost time. He didn't want to lose any more.

"Hey, Mom, over here," Amelia called out.

Ry opened his eyes and looked over his shoulder. The kitchen light cast Ellie in silhouette as she came along the wooden walkway through the dunes.

His heart beat faster, picking up speed as she stepped off the end onto the sand.

Come this way, Ellie. Come to me.

She went to Amelia instead, who sat cross-legged on the other side of the fire, her back propped against Ray's chest. Ray dug around in the cooler with his good hand, brought out a bottle of white and poured a glass for Ellie. She sipped it, casting a casual glance around the circle. Her eyes slid over him, leaving a trail of heat on his skin.

Amelia said something that made her laugh, the sweet sound weaving seamlessly into the fabric of the night, wrapping around him. Homesickness brought a lump to his throat. He was homesick for Boston. But mostly he was homesick for these people. He'd missed all of them. They were the family of his heart, especially the Marones and their men. He loved Ray. Even Cody already felt like a brother.

Ry's chest squeezed. How he envied those guys. They'd each found a Marone and figured out the secret to keeping her.

He wanted that secret, badly.

CHAPTER SEVEN

THE TIDE WAS going out; the beach growing wider. Ryan gazed out past the waves, across the cove to the lights of the Ogunquit hotels, glittering like diamonds strung along the curve of the coastline.

Here in Wells, only houses lined the sleepy shore behind him, their windows casting faint yellow squares that fell far short of the dunes. Down the beach to left and right a few other bonfires flickered, each throwing its own intimate circle of light, making the shadows between them seem even deeper.

Ellie continued to ignore him, which he decided to take as a good sign. It meant he'd gotten to her. She wanted him, and her only defense was to pretend he didn't exist.

His heart lifted as she wandered down to the water's edge, then drifted along the shoreline until she disappeared in the darkness. He waited, eyes glued to the spot where she'd vanished from sight. Long moments passed, and the longer she was gone, the happier he felt. Because Ellie loved a good party, and nothing could keep her away from this one except extreme temptation.

She was fighting it, of course, resisting that temptation with her considerable willpower. But all the while she'd feel his pull, tugging at her clothes, sensitizing her skin as the tension inside her wound tighter, and tighter.

He saw all of it in her stiff shoulders when she came back into view. She telegraphed everything with those shoulders; he'd learned to read them long ago. Right now they cried out for release, the kind only he could give her.

But she wasn't ready to surrender yet. She headed straight for the cooler and filled her glass, then made the rounds, chatting with everyone but him, ignoring him utterly.

As he watched her, his smile grew. Because it took a lot of energy to ignore someone that hard. A lot of attention. He wanted Ellie's attention, and more.

Down the beach, the bonfires began to wink out. Midnight came and went, and finally their own party broke up, people heading out two by two.

The moment of truth had arrived.

Ellie dawdled by the fire, collecting empties. She could have left it to Amelia and Ray, but Ry figured that by now temptation was riding her hard. She couldn't bring herself to leave, so she was trying to wait him out, hoping he'd leave and take temptation with him.

Fat chance. Ellie was stubborn, for sure, but he was stubborner.

He bided his time. First Mike and Kate, then Cody and Julie, offered him a ride back to the hotel. He declined.

He wasn't going anywhere without Ellie.

Finally, they were the last two left on the beach. Even Ray and Amelia had gone off to bed, taking the cooler and offering Ryan a furtive thumbs-up as they called good-night.

Ellie gathered up a stray beach towel, shook it out and threw it over her shoulder, then started to kick sand over the dying fire. With her tiny feet it could take all night to bury it. And Ryan was done waiting.

Pushing up from the sand, he strode toward her. She saw him coming and scooted around to the other side of the fire.

He followed her.

She kept scooting. It was a standoff until he leapt over the fire pit and landed beside her, close enough to pull her into his arms.

But he didn't. He kept his hands to himself. He'd chased her as far as he was going to. The next move was hers, and he was as sure as he could be that she'd make it.

Eventually.

Meanwhile, she propped her fists on her hips and glared up at him, her delicate features limned in gold by the fire's last light. Her brow was a flat line that shadowed her eyes.

"Why are you still here?" she demanded.

"Why are you?"

She spread her arms. "I'm cleaning up, what else? That's what mothers do."

Her way of not-so-subtly making the point that she was a grown-up with kids, while he was still a kid himself. It was one of her old reliable arguments, as ridiculous now as it ever was.

Since he'd already debated the merits with her three years ago to no avail, he went with the obvious instead, did an exaggerated look around at the pristine sand.

"Exactly," she said. "I picked up the bottles, drained the melted ice, and now it's left to me to put out the fire."

As if he hadn't witnessed Cody and Ray and Mike each offer to do so.

"You're so full of shit," he said. "You're still out here because you're waiting for me to jump you."

She snorted loudly.

"Admit it," he went on, "you want what I've got, but you won't take responsibility for going after it. You're waiting for me to seduce you, so you can tell yourself you were drunk and I took advantage."

He shook his head slowly. "I'm not playing that game, Ellie. If you want me, I'm right here. But you'll have to reach out and take me."

ELLIE DUG HER hands deep into the pockets of her cut-offs. She had to, because her fingers itched to grab hold of him. It was criminal how tempting he was, glowing like some ancient god in the firelight.

In fact, the whole damn scene was too primitive, as if they were the last man and woman standing on the edge of the earth at the end of the world, with nothing to keep them from pulling each other down on the sand and making frantic, desperate love to the timeless rhythm of the sea pounding the shore.

That sounds like fun, a little voice piped up in the back of her brain. *Would it be so bad to give in for a night? Just one night to warm yourself up in his fire . . .*

Yes, it would be bad! she shouted back. *Ryan Murphy is addictive. With him, there's no such thing as just one night. That's like a junkie promising herself just one fix. An alcoholic swearing to take just one drink.*

Like those addicts, after her one night with Ryan Ellie would have to start her recovery all over again. Suffer another long, painful withdrawal.

Three years ago, she'd barely held out. A hundred times she'd reached for the phone, brought his number up, hovered over the call button. She'd missed him like a limb, like water or air.

But he's going back to LA after the wedding, the little voice reminded her. *So it's not like you'll have a chance to get involved again.*

Well. That was true.

And this time you know what you're getting into. You can keep your guard up.

Also true. He couldn't sneak up on her this time.

What I'm saying is, it can truly be "just sex."

With Ryan, that meant really good sex with a guy who knew every trick in the book.

You owe it to yourself.

She really did. The wedding weekend was proving to be harder than she'd expected. First, she was semi-losing Kate, which was major. Then Ryan showed up, turning her inside out. Not that she wasn't over him. She was. But still, the weekend should offer at least *some* fun.

Sex with Ryan would be fun.

It would also be trouble. Because Ry had a tendency to take things too seriously. He cared too much. About people, even strangers, which made him a great cop. About puppies and kittens, which made him a great human. And about her, which currently made him a pain in her ass.

And still the sea kept pounding the shore. She wanted to laugh at herself for feeling its primal pull, but it was too real, too powerful to deny.

Yet she tried.

"Pretty full of yourself," she scoffed.

He said nothing in reply, just raised one eyebrow. Damn it. The Rock had nothing on Ry when it came to The Eyebrow.

She should take a step back, put some distance between them. But she had nowhere to go. He'd angled around so the fire pit was behind her, the heat from the embers warming the backs of her legs.

Summoning the last of her willpower, she broke their eyelock and dropped her gaze . . .

To his chest. Oh Lord, his chest. His tight black T-shirt did nothing to conceal his iron pecs and flat stomach.

She stared silently until words of some sort were absolutely required. "Still training, I see." A breathless whisper.

After a long moment of silence, he flexed first one pec, then the other. The old bouncing-pec trick that had always cracked her up.

It couldn't have startled her more, here in the midst of what felt like a life-and-death struggle. Yet it was as irresistible as ever. Laughter bubbled up in her chest, expanding her shriveled lungs, breaching her last defenses.

"Goddamn you, Ryan Murphy." She threw herself at him, arms around his waist, cheek flattened against that fabulous chest. He scooped her in, burying his nose in her hair, laughing against her neck.

"For fuck's sake, El. It took you long enough."

"Long enough is right," she said, pulling back to grab a fistful of black T-shirt. "Quit wasting time and get your clothes off."

She shoved his shirt up, let him lift it the rest of the way off, as she dragged her fingertips down, bumping over his abs, following the happy trail to his shorts. She fumbled with the button, then the zipper, her eager hands shaking.

Before she could finish the job, he lifted his sweatshirt over her head, peeled off her tank, and popped her breasts out of her bra. His hands shook too as he took their weight in his rough palms. When he brought his mouth down, scraping his teeth over one nipple then laving it all better, her mind fuzzed. Oh yeah, he knew what she liked.

Pulling back, he whispered her name, and the ragged desire in his voice inflamed her own need to satisfy him. Hooking her hands in his waistband, she dropped to her knees, dragging his shorts down with her, freeing him. She took a moment, just one, to savor the magnificence that was Ryan, before she reached for him—

"Oh no you don't," he growled, hooking her under the arms and hauling her upright. "I got plans for you, woman."

She snorted a laugh. "I had plans for you too, dummy."

"Mine involve more than a ten-second blow job. Because that's how long I'd last with your mouth on me."

Pleasure shivered over her skin like goose bumps. This wanting, this being wanted, God how she'd missed it. How she craved it.

"I want to play," she said, stroking the flat of her tongue over one fabulous pec, snaking a hand down to the hard-on sandwiched against her stomach, wrapping her palm around it, so hard and so soft, satin over iron.

He groaned, and the vibration as it ran through his chest fired her blood. Ryan was so much better than wine. He was hundred-proof whiskey straight from the bottle.

"You wanna play?" he growled. "We'll play."

He pulled her down on the towel she'd dropped on the sand, kicked his shorts off, and rolled her onto her back in one motion. Hooking one muscled thigh over her legs, he shoved his hand down into her panties, finding her heat. Playing in it.

Her back arched, mind blown. Thoughts devolved to sensation: hard shoulders under her fingernails, hot breath on her neck. Long fingers moving with purpose as she quickly climbed the peak toward . . .

He pulled his hand away. She cried out, tried to shove it back down her shorts. But he was stronger by a mile, shook her off, then ripped her buttonflies wide open.

"Playtime's over," he said roughly.

Shoving her shorts past her knees, he came up over her, balanced on his elbows, staring down at her. Not asking permission, just giving her a brief moment to state any objections.

She was fresh out. Out of patience too. She needed to get back to that peak and start climbing again.

Wrapping her legs around his hips, she pulled him down. He sank into her with a groan, paused again for an instant, maybe for her sake, maybe for his own. Then he pulled back and thrust hard, driving her into the sand, again, and again. She met him head-on, lifting her hips, moving with the rhythm he set, every muscle and tendon tuned into him, turned on to him. Both of them in sync, going deeper, climbing higher.

Consumed in his heat she didn't fight the wave of emotions that swamped her, spilling tears down her temples, sweetening the heat. Ry must have felt it too, how could he not, and he wanted more, demanding it with the palm that jacked up her hips, the fingers that fisted in her hair. "Give it to me," he gritted out through his teeth. "Give me all of it."

She did, working him as hard as he worked her, taking his mouth in a kiss, pouring herself into him, giving him everything, and taking everything from him, until her body shook, and the only thing left was his face an inch above hers, familiar and beloved, holding her together as she came apart beneath him.

CHAPTER EIGHT

WATCHING ELLIE COME stole Ry's breath, flooding him
with pride and possessiveness, and an almost painful
tenderness for the beautiful, uninhibited woman in his
arms.

It also unleashed the most powerful orgasm of his
life.

His heart was still hammering, and full to brim,
when he finally recovered enough strength to push up
onto his palms and gaze down at her in the fire's last
light. He broke into a smile. Her eyes were unfocused.
She was tousled and spacey, and totally, irresistibly
fuckable.

Hoping her endorphin hangover would last all night,
he rolled off of her onto his side, leaving one arm across
her stomach, his palm curled around her waist. God,
it felt good to hold her again. He pressed his lips to her

shoulder, and slowly, like she was waking up from a long lazy nap, she rolled her head toward him.

He brought his hand up, traced her cheek with his fingertips. The crescent moon hung low on the horizon, and the embers were nothing but a few orange coals, but that was plenty of light. He already knew every angle of her face. In three years it hadn't changed much. An extra crease or two around her eyes, a laugh line parenthesizing her lips. Those things were precious to him.

That's what she didn't understand. He loved that she'd lived, that she'd fought her way back from widowhood, raised two fabulous daughters single-handedly. That she'd put herself through college, become a teacher, and devoted so much of herself to her students that when she'd been promoted to high-school principal, two decades' worth of tenth-graders had come back to Newton to throw a surprise party for her.

She'd earned every line with worry and laughter, and she'd earn a hell of a lot more before she was done. He wanted to be there for that. He wanted to share his lines with her too, to earn them together.

He skimmed the curve of her jaw, said her name like a prayer. "Ellie."

She blinked languidly.

With the pad of his thumb, he rubbed her soft lips. They parted and he pushed in, between her teeth, until he found the tip of her tongue, warm and wet.

"Ellie, my love." The barest whisper. And his biggest mistake.

He should've known. The L-word brought her brain back online. She blinked again. Her eyes widened.

She spit out his thumb.

Panic gripped him. Instinctively, he dropped his hand to her breast. It worked before; it might work again.

Nope. She wriggled away from him, off the towel. Her bare ass hit the sand and she yipped, rolling up on her side, giving him an eyeful of perfect ass.

He grabbed it with both hands.

"Keep off the ass," she snapped out, and he laughed. If she could joke, maybe all wasn't lost.

As she wrestled with the shorts that dangled from one of her ankles, he hooked a finger through a belt loop. "Maybe you should leave 'em off," he said, tugging down while she tugged up.

"Let go, will ya, before I get sand in my hoohaa."

"Good point," he said, releasing the loop. "We'll take this to my room. Mike's sleeping at Kate's. We'll have it all to ourselves."

"Thanks, but I've got my own room," she bit out.

"Or that," he said agreeably.

"I mean," she said, pushing up onto her knees, tucking her tits down into her bra, "you go to your room, I'll go to mine, and when we wake up tomorrow we can pretend this was just a bad dream."

"It's a little late for buyer's remorse," he said.

"It's never too late for remorse." She found her tank, shook out the sand. "I've been remorseful for three years."

"For sending me away?"

"For getting involved with you in the first place." She clambered to her feet and glowered down at him, fists on her hips.

He played his last card. Rolling onto his back, he locked his hands behind his head and shamelessly showed off the goods. He was already half hard from watching her wriggle around getting dressed. He grew another two inches under her furious gaze.

It gave her pause, as he'd hoped it would. Instead of storming off like she'd obviously intended, she stood as still as a pillar growing out of the sand. He could almost hear the clash of swords as she fought a bloody war with herself.

Languidly, he bent one knee, tilted it out just a little, all the better to frame his package.

A long moment passed silently, fraught with tension that he did a better job of hiding than she did.

Then, "You're a jerk, Ry," she squeezed out between her teeth. "You're a jerk, and I hate your guts!"

Still she stood there.

"If you hate me so much," he drawled out, "why don't you come down here and fuck me to death."

"Aghh!" she howled, shaking her fists at the moon.

Then she tore her shirt over her head and fell on him.

CHAPTER NINE

ELLIE SLITTED ONE eye open. Sand and sea, and a barely dawn sky glowing pale green just above the horizon.

Apparently she'd slept on the beach. Not the first time, but the first time in a long time.

The hard, heavy groin warming her backside could only be Ryan's. He'd tucked her under his chest, sheltering her like a lean-to built of muscle and bone. His big arm hugged her close and she'd wound her own arms around it, snuggling it to her chest. Her toes were tucked between his calves. Given that the temperature had fallen during the night, she was warmer than she had a right to be. He'd thrown his sweatshirt over them, but all the heat was coming from behind her.

She sighed, envisioning problems. Ry was bound to make more of this than it was: a simple roll on the beach.

Well, make that three rolls on the beach. Three hot, sweaty, incredible rolls.

God, he'd ground her into the sand. She'd never get it all out of her hair, or her crack, for that matter. Not to mention that there was a good reason sand was used to make sandpaper.

Overhead a seagull circled, an early riser scoping out the beach for party leftovers. He dropped down on the sand a few feet away, cawed his displeasure at her thorough cleanup job.

Behind her, Ryan stirred.

All of him stirred.

Her genius brain told her to push his big carcass off of her and get out of there. But her body had other ideas. She wriggled against him.

"Mmm," he purred in her ear like a big cat.

"Mmm," she purred back like a kitten.

He cuddled her tighter. She snuggled into him deeper.

How they got from cuddling and snuggling to her straddling him she couldn't quite recall, but somehow she found herself staring down into his eyes, her palms flat on his chest, his biceps flexing as he lifted her onto him.

She settled, taking a moment, savoring the feel of him hot and hard inside her. Then leaning into her palms, she rocked forward. Pushed back.

His jaw tightened. A muscle jumped in his cheek.

She smiled. He was so pretty. The sky had lightened to pink, and the glow gilded his skin. She soaked up the sight. After all, if she was going to have meaningless sex, she should get the most out of it, right?

Sitting back slowly, she dragged her fingertips down over the ridges of his abs. Her gaze flicked to his face again. He watched her through narrowed eyes, his full lips pulled taut, his passion chained as she toyed with him. Patient.

Until he wasn't.

Then he took charge, took her over, lifting her, pulling her down to meet his thrusts, working her, working her. She surrendered control, let him have his way with her until it was too much and not enough all at once. Then she threw herself into it too, riding him, riding him, every atom of her body and soul joined with every atom of his.

Another orgasm rushed toward her, almost within reach. She threw back her head, braced her arms. And— what the *hell*!—something icy prodded her buttock, so shocking that she somersaulted right over Ry's head.

ELLIE'S CHEEKS WERE still burning as she and Ryan tiptoed along the side of Amelia and Ray's house and made for her Mustang, parked on the street.

She'd left the top down, and dew stippled the seats. She didn't pause to dry them, just hopped in and cranked the ignition as Ry flopped in the passenger seat. "That was fun," he said, still laughing it up. He hadn't quit since she'd done the fastest cowgirl dismount in rodeo history.

"Fun for you," she grumbled, shifting into drive. "You got off. I got the world's coldest nose in the ass." There'd been no chance to recapture the mood either, not with Jester the beady-eyed dachshund yipping a circle around them until his eighty-five-year-old owner finally towed him away.

"Don't worry, babe." Ry reached over and brushed sand off her thigh, then covered her cool skin with his warm hand. "I'll take care of you when we get back."

"Like hell." She hit the gas, the tires spinning in the thin film of sand on the pavement. "That was a one-off, Ry."

"My point exactly," he said. "I was the one that got off. Now it's your turn." His pinky slid up under the edge of her shorts.

She shook her leg but he clung like a spider.

She squealed to a stop and jumped out of the Mustang.

"Hey!" He checked over his shoulder for traffic, but it was the ass crack of dawn. They were the only car on the street.

She circled around, yanked his door open. "Drive," she said. That would keep his hands busy.

He gave her a surly stare. Surly and stupidly sexy, with lids half lowered over eyes as blue as the sky.

"Or walk," she added, resolutely ignoring the seductive scruff on his cheeks.

She must've looked as weak as she felt, because he did one of his long, slow smiles, the kind that traveled from the right side of his mouth to the left while turtles walked across Galapagos, and stars were born and went super-nova, and her heart beat a hundred thousand beats.

"You wouldn't kick me out," he said easily. "Not after, what, at least seven orgasms."

"In a New York minute, buster." So what if his wrinkled T-shirt still had her handprints pressed into it? She had it in her to leave him on the side of the road. Oh yes she did.

He heaved a great sigh, swung one leg out of the car. Then the other. Unfolded his frame from the bucket seat and spent a long moment towering over her.

She stared up at him, unflinching.

"You're losing your shorts," he said.

"Damn it!" Her now-buttonless buttonflies had slid halfway down her butt.

"Not that I mind," he said as he circled the car. "But you might give Jester's pop another heart attack." He tipped his head toward the sound of shuffling feet behind her, but she refused to look.

"Just drive," she hissed, dropping into the seat. "And get me some coffee before I completely lose my shit."

CHAPTER TEN

RYAN HIT THE Dunkie's drive-thru, badly in need of caffeine himself. If he'd slept for two hours, he'd be surprised. Ellie's stamina hadn't suffered any since the last time he'd had her under him.

She was, and always would be, everything he wanted in bed.

Out of bed too, though he wasn't going there with her yet. The timing was wrong. She was too busy stewing. Probably berating herself for giving in to him, and worrying—correctly—that he'd try to level up from friends-with-benefits to a full-blown relationship.

That's why she was blowing him off. She foresaw the dreaded "complications." So he had to keep the focus on sex. Pretend that was all he was after, so she'd keep giving it to him, and giving it to him, all while he worked his way under her armor.

Propping his forearm on the window frame, he steered with two fingers, used his free hand to bring some kind of order to his hair.

"Nice day," he observed casually. "Almost as nice as LA."

She sniffed derisively, the typical Bostonian's reaction to anything left coast.

He smirked. "Of course, *we* have this weather year-round." *We*, as if he was all-California now.

"I like the change of seasons," she said stiffly, every New Englander's rote response to wimps who couldn't take winter.

"I used to say the same thing," he replied, smug and condescending.

That annoyed her, as intended. "I'm sure it's more than the weather," she sniffed. "It's the sun-streaked blondes."

He smiled a cocky-bastard smile and let curiosity eat away at her.

"No girlfriend?" she asked when she finally couldn't help it.

He favored her with an eyebrow. "Would I have done what we just did if I had a girlfriend?"

"You never know."

"*You* know. You know *me*." She needed to remember that.

She lifted a shoulder. "People change."

"Have you?"

"Of course I've changed."

Well, shit, did that mean she was still involved? "I thought you dumped the jock," he said, trying to sound like it wasn't a matter of life and death.

"He's a personal trainer," Ellie said sharply, "and it was mutual."

Relief made him reckless. He snorted a laugh. "It's never mutual with you, Ellie. You're a heartbreaker."

"Grow up, Ryan. Not everyone's after a white picket fence."

He nodded sagely. "So that was your problem with me. I'm too traditional. Too suburban."

"If you're starting that again, pull over and I'll get out right here." She pointed at a Trolley Stop sign.

He kept driving.

She crossed her arms tightly under her breasts, apparently unaware that it practically pushed them right out of her top. They clung to decency by the tips of their nipples.

He fisted his hand to keep from stuffing it down her shirt. Now wasn't the time to get distracted by nipples. They were coming into Ogunquit, and traffic was picking up. Cars, bicycles, joggers pushing strollers. Pedestrians crossing everywhere but at crosswalks.

He glued his eyes to the road. Did damage control.

"Listen," he said, infusing California casual into his voice, "I'm not trying to dredge up old times. I'm just here for the weekend, looking for a good time." He eased his shoulders, disguising it as a shrug. "So we've got a past, so what? It doesn't have to ruin our fun, right?"

Her head turned his way. He felt her studying him, assessing.

He knew it was what she wanted to hear, or at least what she *thought* she wanted to hear, so he laid on more of the same, glancing over at her with a half smile calculated to appear artless, playful, and uncomplicatedly sexy.

It was a lot to ask from one half smile. He returned his eyes to the road while it did its work. Waited breathlessly while appearing to be absorbed in the scenery.

A few minutes later she uncrossed her arms. He let a sigh of relief trickle out silently between his lips.

She lifted her cup from the holder, picked at the edge of the plastic lid with her fingernail. "Sorry," she said at last. "It's . . . a weird weekend. And this was a weird night."

He nodded. "Sex on the beach. It's not just a happy-hour drink anymore."

She chuckled. Then she laughed. So did he, and felt the wall between them start to crumble.

"Oh God," she said, wiping her eyes, "what if Amelia had found us?"

"Lifelong therapy, that's what. But the upside for Ray is she'd have learned some new moves."

She groan-laughed, a unique-to-Ellie sound he hadn't heard in way too long.

Reaching over, he plucked the cup from her hand, took a slug, and passed it back to her as naturally as if they'd done it a thousand times, which they had.

"Meanwhile, that old guy—" he began.

"That old *perv*, you mean. I was just thinking about him, and in hindsight—"

He cracked up. "*Hind*sight. Get it?"

"Very punny. What I meant was, in *reflecting on* our encounter with him, I'm starting to believe that if his little yapper hadn't tried to make it a three-way, he would've kept on watching."

"Of course he would've. He's old, but he's a man."

"So if that had been you—"

"Hell yeah. Asses like yours don't pop up every day—"

"My ass didn't *pop up*."

"Uh, yeah, it did. A bunch of times."

The withering look she spared him couldn't disguise her own half smile. She waved a hand to the left. "Don't miss the turnoff."

He drove onto the hotel grounds and parked in the spot outside of her room.

She hopped out, came around, and opened his door. "Out. And make it snappy, before Julie gets an eyeful."

He took his time unlimbering each leg from the low-slung seat. As soon as he was out, she was in, hitting the button to put the top up. He stood there waiting for her, faking nonchalance while every cell in his body jangled, primed to race to her room and finish what Jester had so rudely interrupted.

The roof dropped into place and she snapped the snaps, then stuck her head out. "What are you still doing here?"

"Waiting for you, what else?"

"Gee, thanks, but I can find my room all by myself. That one's yours, right there." She pointed next door.

So that's how she wanted to play it. His turn to cross his arms. "I'm not going to my room. I'm going to yours, and I'm gonna get you off—"

"Shhh!" She leapt out of the car and slapped a hand over his mouth, swiveling her head furtively.

There wasn't much to see at this ungodly hour, just two groundskeepers mopping dew off the Adirondack chairs that were ranged around the lawn, and a trio of joggers trotting toward the path to the beach. The remainder of Sunrise Bluff's guests continued to slumber.

Ryan was willing to wake every one of them if that's what it took to get into her room.

He licked her palm.

She yanked it back. "Ew! Quit it."

"Just practicing for—"

"Shh!" She shoved him up the steps and onto the porch, tried prodding him toward his room, but he pivoted around her and planted himself in front of her door.

"Scram," she whispered.

"Uh-uh." Full volume.

"I mean it, Ryan." Barely moving her lips.

"So do I." Louder.

"You're gonna wake everyone up!"

"That's up to you." He lowered his voice. "We've got unfinished business, Ellie. I'm for going inside and

Her formerly taut thighs had gained some dimples. And her already lopsided breasts had lost some of their perk. Moonlight might have concealed her imperfections from Ryan, but even the tiniest pimple couldn't hide from the bathroom's fluorescent glare.

Turning in the doorway, she faced him head-on. And God, he looked great. Tousled and rumpled and already getting naked. He'd dropped his sweatshirt on the floor—another puddle of sand—and was peeling his T-shirt over his head.

As they rose, her eyes ate up the acres of hard-body. No pooch on him. No dimples, no droop. He was all suntanned male in the prime of his life. If he'd been anyone but Ryan, she would've counted her blessings, dragged him into the shower, and gone to town on that gorgeousness.

But Ryan was different, goddamn it. She didn't want him to be. With all her heart she wished he were just a sweet, friendly guy to have fun with. A new relationship, a new lover. Not an ex who'd remember three-years-ago Ellie, and who'd now see that her body was going downhill on roller skates.

Damn you, Ryan, why couldn't you stay in LA?

She dragged her gaze up to his face—more perfection—his cheeks shadowed with stubble and mouthwateringly masculine, his full lips slowly curving in a fuck-me-dead smile. His blue eyes on fire and filled with—wait, what now? Was that *emotion* lurking under the flames?

She pointed at the door. "Out."

The bedroom smile slid off his face. "But . . . sex!"

Maybe if that's all it was, just sex, she could've lived with the embarrassment of her deteriorating body. But no way was she getting tangled up in *emotions*.

She scooped up his sweatshirt, pushed it into his chest. "Go away, Ryan."

"Why?" He spread his arms. "We're as good together as we ever were. Better."

"I'm not interested."

"In sex?" he scoffed. "Since when?"

"Since now." She stuffed a wad of sweatshirt into his waistband. "Take your perfect bod and get gone."

For a long moment he studied her. She felt him testing her resolve. Hopefully he wouldn't sense how weak it was, how one more push would crumble it.

He didn't push. Instead, he tugged the sweatshirt from his shorts and looped it around his neck like a towel.

"I'll see you later, Ellie," he said, and then he walked out her door, his neutral tone and bland expression leaving her with no idea whether he was giving up on her, or simply deferring his next assault on her defenses.

She should hope for the former. But as the door closed behind him, loneliness settled over her, and the pretty room she'd found so cozy before felt vast and empty and hollow.

THE *LADY ARABELLA* boasted a suntanned crew of six, each of the cheerful young men and women dressed in a polo so white the reflected sunlight would've burned out Ryan's sleep-deprived retinas if not for his Ray-Bans.

Slumped in his chair at the table for eight, feeling the very opposite of cheerful, he watched with minimal interest as they divided the duties of sailing the fifty-four-foot yacht and clearing away the remnants of his party's gourmet breakfast.

The happy couple stood hand-in-hand on the port side, staring not out over the glittering Atlantic, but into each other's eyes, annoyingly blissful.

At the far end of the table Cody lolled complacently in his seat, face tipped to the sun, looking like a glossy magazine ad for expensive cologne or rugged ten-thousand-dollar watches.

"The guy's indestructible." The disgruntled murmur issued from Ray. He was seated beside Ryan, a Red Sox cap snugged down low on his forehead. "Drank more than I did by a gallon, and look at him." He slanted a narrow eye at Cody, his carefully modulated tone attesting to his own throbbing head.

"I'd like to hate him," Ryan said in solidarity. "But he's too fucking nice."

Rubbing his bristly jaw, Ryan sat up straighter, well aware that he looked like five miles of bad road. Not that Ellie would've noticed. She'd captivated the captain, who'd already shown her every inch of the stupid boat and was now regaling her with tales of his sailing heroics. As if breakfast cruises along the Maine shoreline took a lot of enemy fire.

He forced his attention back to Ray. "So I guess you and Amelia slept in?" he asked just to make sure the old perv was the only witness.

"I did," Ray said, "but Amelia didn't really drink much. She was up and at 'em at her usual ungodly hour."

Uh-oh. "She's an early riser, huh? Did she, uh, get out for a walk on the beach?"

"I don't know, she's been kind of quiet this morning."

Ryan scratched his chin. Come to think of it, Amelia hadn't said a word to him since they'd boarded.

"But she's sure giving Jules an earful about something," Ray added with a glance at the sisters, huddled together in the bow. "I'm sure I'll hear about it later."

Uh-oh.

"It's probably nothing. You know how sisters are." Ryan tried to sound offhand, like he was an expert on sisters, which he wasn't, having none of his own.

As if they'd heard his ill-fated words, both of them swiveled their heads and locked on to him with tractor beams. Casually, he looked away, trying to break their hold.

"Hey, Ry," Julie called across the deck.

He pretended not to hear.

"Ry!" A shout he couldn't ignore.

Still he tried to deflect it, lifting his mimosa in salute, as if he thought they were just calling a friendly hello.

Julie beckoned. Ryan stalled.

"Dude, I hate to tell you," Ray said, "but you're being summoned."

sneer. "According to Amelia, you've got nothing to be embarrassed about."

He shot a glance at Amelia. Her face was red as an apple. "You oughta be ashamed of yourself," he said to her.

She mustered defiance. "At least I wasn't boinking on the beach at the crack of dawn!"

"But you were spying on people who were boinking on the beach," he said. "Which is way worse, if you ask me."

"Nobody's asking you," Julie put in. "What we're doing is telling you: do not—and I mean it, Ry—do *not* break Mom's heart again."

The injustices kept piling up. "I told you before, I didn't break her heart. She broke mine."

Julie fanned away reason and rationality with a wave of her hand. "You *left*, Ryan. You should've stayed. You should've kept working on her. She *loved* you."

"And I loved her, Jules. I still do." He dropped his voice, but frustration had his teeth grinding. "If you want to lecture somebody on heartbreak, go pry her away from Captain America and ask her how it feels to use me all night and kick me out on my ass this morning."

Julie dropped his shirt and took a half step back. "TMI, Ry. TMI."

"Says the woman who just got my performance review. *From her sister.*"

Amelia held up her hand. "Hang on. I didn't give her any details, she's making that up."

"And I'm supposed to be grateful for that?" He glowered down at her, feigning belligerence when he actually felt like squirming. "Just how long did you stand there watching?"

"I didn't," she cried. "I ran straight back in the house to bleach my eyes."

For a short, silent moment, he favored them both with a scowl as he considered his next move. They seemed semi-repentant, so if he played his cards right maybe he could bring them over to his side of the field. He could sure use the help.

Dropping the scowl, he shoved his hands in his pockets and leaned a hip against the rail. "The last thing in the world I want to do is hurt Ellie," he said. "But I can't seem to make her understand."

"Understand what?" Julie asked.

"That she's worried about stupid stuff."

Amelia and Julie exchanged identical he-did-not-just-say-that looks.

With exaggerated restraint, Amelia said, "The way to a woman's heart is *not* by telling her she's worried about *stupid stuff.*"

He had to agree that Ellie never took it very well.

"Exactly what stupid stuff are you referring to?" Amelia went on.

"The age difference, what else?" He rolled his eyes. "Nine years. It's not like she could be my mother, for god's sake."

Julie pursed her lips, staring down at the deck while Amelia did her tolerant-of-toddlers voice. "It so happens I agree with you about that. But given society's hang-ups about older women and younger men, it's not *stupid* for her to be concerned about it."

"Sure it is—"

"Shut up," Julie hissed. "Just shut up and listen for a minute." She drew a deep breath, settled herself down. "You need to realize," she went on, "that it's Mom who'll take the brunt of it. *She'll* be the target of the snide, passive-aggressive remarks."

"So she's afraid of being teased?" That would be uncomfortable for sure, but it didn't seem like a good enough reason to deny herself decades of his love and goddamned devotion.

Julie's patience slipped. "It goes to the heart of her self-esteem, dummy. Aging isn't the same for women. It's not fair, it's not particularly enlightened, but the sad truth is that our self-image is, to a large degree, based on our ability to attract men."

He cast a bitter eye toward the obviously infatuated captain, mooning over Ellie as she preened daintily under her oversized straw sunhat. "Attracting men's not exactly a problem for her."

Amelia dunce-slapped him.

"Ow!" He rubbed the side of his head.

"I thought SWAT required a high IQ," she said. "Did you cheat on the test?"

"I'm smart," he said defensively, feeling anything but.

"You lack *emotional* intelligence," Julie informed him. "Maybe you can analyze tactics and strategies, but you're dumb as a stump when it comes to Mom."

"Then help me." He spread his hands. "Tell me what to do."

"First of all," Amelia said, "you need to stop fixating on the surface, and dig deeper. Yes, Mom is worried about the age difference. She's thinking that when she's fifty, you'll barely be into your forties. When she's sixty, you'll be just a few years older than she is now—"

He held up a hand. "You all think I'm a shallow son of a bitch, don't you? That it's all about the sex."

Both girls went green around the gills, but he was in too deep to spare them.

"Yeah, it's good," he said. "It's goddamn amazing."

Amelia went greener.

"But it's not just the sex," he said. "I love *her*. I love the way her brain works. The connections she makes that seem wacky until you think about them and then they seem brilliant. I love her non sequiturs—"

"Well, you're alone on that one," Julie cut in. "But okay, we get it. The thing is"—she took a tight grip on his arm, like she meant to drill her point in with her fingertips—"you're still stuck on the surface. Mom's real problem is—"

"Oh *shit!*" The cry came from Ellie as the wind caught her hat and spun it off into the sailboat's wake.

CHAPTER THIRTEEN

EVERY MUSCLE IN Ryan's body tensed into rescue mode. He stepped toward the rail.

"Absolutely not," Julie growled, clutching his arm tighter. "You are *not* diving into the ocean to save a stupid hat."

"But—"

Amelia clung to his other arm. "Mom won't think it's heroic, Ry. She'll think it's dumb."

His body jerked reflexively, all his instincts telling him to save the hat, save the hat.

"For God's sake, Ryan," Julie forced through clenched teeth. "This is exactly what we're trying to explain to you. Mom's afraid of you dying. The last thing you should do is prove to her that you're reckless enough to break your neck for a hat."

He forgot about the hat. "Wait, what? She's afraid of me *dying*?"

"In the line. Just like Dad."

"Well, for fuck's sake." His weight shifted back on his heels, like he'd taken a right hook to the jaw.

Or a hammer to his helmet.

He dropped his gaze to the deck, but it wasn't the gleaming boards or coiled lines that he saw. It was the twisted lips and burning eyes of a deadbeat dad who thought the world had done him wrong and who meant to find justice by gutting his ex in front of their two-year-old son.

Ry had known what he was getting into when he kicked in the kitchen door. Domestic situations were the most unpredictable. The most dangerous.

He'd thought he was on top of it. Had eyes on the dad where he'd cornered the mom in the living room. Knew the kid was hiding behind the ratty recliner.

What he didn't know—what nobody knew—was that the dad's latest girlfriend was on the scene too.

She'd been busy tossing the bedroom, as if the destitute victim had anything worth stealing. When Ryan burst into the kitchen, she grabbed a hammer from the counter and brought it down on his head like he was a nail she meant to drive through the floor. His helmet cracked like an egg and he went down in a puddle. If not for the rest of his team storming in right behind him, the crazy tweaker would've beaten him to paste while he lay there unconscious.

When he woke up two days later, his CO was standing over his hospital bed. "You've been working too hard," he told Ryan. "My fault, I shouldn't have kept approving the overtime. But you're on paid leave now, so find yourself a nice, quiet beach, get yourself laid and blown, and I'll see you in a month."

So far so good. Just last night he'd gotten laid and blown on a nice, quiet beach, and he felt better than he'd felt in three years. He wasn't happy about waiting a whole month to get back on the job, but he wasn't worried in the least about dying.

Besides, he said like it was obvious, "Everyone dies eventually."

"Exactly," Amelia said, as if he'd finally seen the light. Which he definitely had not.

"What am I missing?" he said. "I'm not tracking you here. Because if everyone dies eventually . . ." He churned his hand, hoping for clarification.

Julie massaged her temple. "You said it yourself, Ry. Mom makes connections. She connects love and husbands with death and heartache."

Seriously? "But you two are married. She seems good with that."

"I didn't say her connections are always consistent or make sense to the rest of us. But they do to her." Julie shrugged helplessly. "Maybe she's superstitious, or thinks she's jinxed. Whatever it is, she's sure that if she gets married again, her husband will die and she won't be able to survive it."

"Thus the younger men," Amelia added. "She thinks she won't be tempted to fall in love and marry a guy who's ten years her junior."

"Are you saying it's not the age difference per se?" he asked, trying to sort through Ellie's neuroses. "It's just a defense against falling in love?"

"Something like that."

"So there's hope." His chest expanded, his first deep breath of the day. "I can't change my age, but maybe I can change her mind."

"I keep telling you it's not that simple," Julie said. "It's all intertwined, and the reason the age difference is an effective defense is because it's a legit concern. Add to that the fact that you're a cop—SWAT, no less—and the whole thing becomes impossible."

He clutched his pounding skull.

Amelia let out a sympathetic sigh. "It goes back to what you said before. Everybody dies."

"So me being younger than her should be a good thing," he said, grasping at straws. "She's more likely to die before me." A gut-wrenching thought that he couldn't believe he was putting in the plus column.

Julie was already shaking her head. "If you bring logic to this party, my man, I guarantee you'll go home alone."

He shoved a hand through his hair and looked out to sea, where sunlight danced happily on the water's surface, oblivious to his churning brain.

"It shouldn't be this hard," he muttered. "I love her, and that should be enough."

The girls were quiet for a moment. Then Julie said, tentatively, "Don't give up."

He turned to her. "I thought you wanted me to lay off so she doesn't get hurt."

Julie glanced at Amelia, who gently touched his arm. "I think maybe we were wrong about that," Amelia said. "If anyone can get through to her, Ry, it's you."

"She's denied herself love for thirty years," Julie said. "But honestly, I don't think she's ever met anyone who tempted her. Except you."

"She deserves you," Amelia added. "And even though I've been mad at you for three years, I think you might *possibly* be worthy of her too."

CHAPTER FOURTEEN

ELLIE PLOPPED ONTO the love seat in her small suite and tried to just breathe.

It was hard, just breathing, knowing that Ryan was next door. How was she supposed to relax when she could feel his heartbeat through the wall?

And what a heart he had. It was too big for one man, so he opened it to everyone, took on their drama and trauma. Protected the weak, rescued the defenseless. He couldn't help it; he had a hero complex. Why, the damn fool had been two seconds away from diving into the drink for her hat!

The instant it hit the water she'd known what he'd do. She'd even spun around to head him off. But she was too far away—on purpose, because she really needed to keep her distance from him.

If her girls hadn't tackled him, the Coast Guard

could be fishing him out of the Atlantic right now, with her hat clutched in his lifeless hand.

What an idiot.

She let her head fall back. Her eyelids drooped as the long night caught up to her. Thank God most of her matron of honor duties were behind her. The bridal shower, arranging dinner, chartering the breakfast cruise. The only things left were hair and makeup, and the wedding. Then she was off duty.

This wedding stuff was hard work . . .

Knuckles on her door woke her with a start. Through the peephole Ryan's unshaven face looked back at her.

"What now?" she called through the door.

"I need some shampoo."

She rolled her eyes. "Use the hotel shampoo. In the little bottle on the sink."

"I don't like the smell. I want to use yours. The lemony one."

Back when they were together he'd always used her products. He liked having the scent on him, he said, because it reminded him of her all through the day.

She pressed her palms to the door, as if he were pushing against it and she had to hold him back. "I don't use that one anymore."

"Baloney. I smelled it."

Of course. He'd had his nose in her hair all night.

She took her eye from the peephole. Dragged a hand through her hair, stiff as a board from the salt spray on the boat.

Against her better judgment, she opened the door.

"Hey, how's it going?" he said, as if they hadn't just had a whole conversation through the door. Then he smiled, and her heart squeezed. Her lungs shrank up, airless. That's how good he looked to her. He actually stole her breath away.

Leaving him in the doorway, she marched toward the bathroom. Behind her, she heard him come inside and close the door.

"Don't make yourself comfortable," she called, a waste of breath, because when she came out with the bottle she found him flopped on the love seat.

"I'm pooped," he said, gazing up at her from under lids that looked as heavy as hers felt.

"That's what you get for staying out all night." She tossed the bottle at him.

He snagged it like a shortstop. "You must be tired too. Let's take a nap."

"Good idea."

He perked up.

"I'll take mine here," she went on, "and you take yours over there." She pointed at the wall.

He grimaced. "I was thinking—"

"I know what you were thinking." Because she was thinking it too. The difference was, she had no intention of acting on it. She pointed at the wall again.

He pushed himself to his feet as though he scarcely had the strength.

She wasn't buying it. Not with those arms, those abs . . .

It dawned on her then that he wasn't wearing a shirt. She pursed her lips. Very sneaky of him to advertise his assets like that. He knew her weakness and wasn't afraid to exploit it.

He was dangerous, Ryan Murphy.

She took a step back.

He took a step forward.

"Ryan," she said, a warning.

"Ellie," he said, a caress.

One big hand lifted. His knuckles brushed her jawline, grazed her earlobe. Fingertips slid into her hair, scratched her scalp lightly.

His touch was magical, tracing fire on her skin, lighting her up. He'd always had this effect. Nothing had changed. Her body still cried out for him. Her heart, her foolish heart, cried his name.

Another step, and his arm came around her waist, tugging her against him, so big, and so hard. She felt tiny, minute. He squeezed her gently, a powerful man controlling his power. It could have made her feel weak, but instead she felt stronger. His belief in her had always given her superpowers.

Now she felt that familiar rush again and, recklessly, impulsively, she curled her arms around his neck. Yes, she was strong, strong enough to take what she wanted. And in this moment what she wanted was Ryan.

The bed was across the room, too far away, so they tumbled to the floor, stripping each other, on fire. Then he was inside her again, all the way in, body and soul, and she gasped his name, raking his shoulders as he rocked her. And when it was over and they'd collapsed in a sweaty and rug-burned heap, Ellie's heart sang a song it hadn't sung in three years.

It sounded suspiciously like a love song.

THEY DOZED OFF on the floor, Ellie tucked against Ry's side. Not the most comfortable place for a nap, but he'd take it over a featherbed with anyone else.

Needless to say, it was too good to last. Ellie woke and went stiff, then made to get up.

He tried to dissuade her by snuggle-rubbing his beard along her cheek, a move that had never failed to melt her like chocolate. And it actually seemed to work at first. She softened slightly as his lips found her ear, the delicate hollow behind it. "Mmm," he hummed, savoring her scent. She was lemon and sea salt and everything Ellie . . .

She pinched her shoulder to her ear. "Quit it. That tickles."

He licked her cheek.

"I mean it, Ry." She tried to wiggle away, so he rolled on top of her. He'd squish her if he had to, just to hold her in place. Because he wasn't ready to let her go. He'd never be ready.

He pushed his hand down between them. "I'm not

done with you," his caveman growled. A gratifying shiver ran through her whole body, an unmistakably primal response. "Open up, babe," he rumbled.

She opened up.

He wore her out.

Wore her down too. This time when he rolled onto his back, breathing hard, staring blindly at the ceiling, she rolled with him without prodding. Using his shoulder as a pillow, she rested her hand on his chest and breathed out a contented sigh.

He smiled fiercely. Damn, she'd made him work for it, but with her fingertips threaded lightly through his chest hair, not quite tickling, but standing every nerve on end, he knew he'd finally dented her armor.

Lifting one heavy hand off the floor, he traced a pattern on her arm—their initials, though he'd never admit something so corny out loud.

Her palm flattened over his heart. "You're such a sap." The chuckle in her voice said she was onto him.

He switched to a random sequence of letters. She chuckled some more.

Pushing up on one elbow, she craned her neck to see the clock. "It's after one. Kate'll be here any minute to drag me to the hairdresser."

He slid his hand up her arm, curled it gently around her shoulder. "Dance with me," he said. "At the reception. Just me, all night."

Her green eyes went soft, then sad. "I don't think—"

"That's good," he cut in. "Don't think. Just say 'yes,

Ryan, I'll dance with you until midnight, and then I'll take you back to my room and fuck you every way I can think of until we fall down unconscious.'"

Her head tilted. "That started out romantic, but somehow it ended up porn."

He grinned. "It can be both."

"Actually it can't." She pushed up onto her knees. "We can do porn, Ry. But romance is off the table."

He wanted to argue. Oh boy, did he want to argue about that.

But clearly there was more work to be done before she laid down her arms. So instead, he said, "Fine. Porn it is."

She'd braced a foot and started to stand, but his words stopped her in mid-crouch.

"You're still okay with just sex?" she asked, eyeing him doubtfully.

Her breasts dangled above his chest. He helped himself to two handfuls. "If you can do it," he said, "so can I."

The biggest lie he'd ever told.

CHAPTER FIFTEEN

ELLIE KNEW IT was weird of her, but damn it, she dreaded the hair/nails/makeup routine most women dreamed of.

"Don't act so put upon," Julie said, wiggling pink toes in the next lounger. "Nobody forced you into this."

"Not true," Kate called from across the room. "I forced her. My wedding photos, my call. Besides," she added with a smirk, "you'd think Ellie would want to doll herself up for—"

Ellie cranked up her headphones, letting Adele drown out the teasing. She could still see it, though, her daughters and Kate yukking it up over "Beach Blanket Bingo," as Kate had dubbed the morning's *in flagrante delicto* adventure.

Fortunately, Ryan had warned her that Amelia had outed them. He'd had some laughs of his own over

Amelia's green gills—which she'd apparently recovered from, seeing as how she was going zinger for zinger with her sister, all at her mother's expense.

Ellie was the only one who didn't find the whole episode sidesplitting.

Julie leaned over and, being elaborately careful of her nails, lifted one side of Ellie's headphones. "Come on, Mom, it's nothing to be embarrassed about. Oh wait, yes it is!"

Hardee har har.

More Adele, please. Louder.

She closed her eyes so she wouldn't have to see their hilarity . . . and next thing she knew, the stylist was shaking her awake. "You're up," she said, hustling Ellie over to the chair.

After draping her in a see-through plastic tent, she stood behind Ellie and started fiddling with her hair. "So, what are you thinking? We can put it up," the perky blonde offered, gathering Ellie's hair in a loose twist. "Or you can wear it down," spreading it over her shoulders. "Maybe with some big waves. Very sexy."

A wolf whistle from Kate. "Sexy! That's what she wants. She's got a hot night ahead of her."

The girls chimed in. Ellie tuned them out. "Do whatever's quickest," she told Perky, "so I can get outta here."

"Okay, the waves it is. Now just sit back and relax. And don't worry about . . ." A sympathetic chin tilt at the mirror. "Our makeup artist is a genius."

Ouch. Ellie focused on her reflection, sort of blurry because she'd taken out her contacts before she left the hotel, and her glasses were now tucked in her purse. Even so, she saw enough to grasp the scale of the crisis—pasty complexion, raccoon eyes, dried-out lips. Gone were the days of staying up all night and still looking dewy fresh in the morning.

Ryan's vision must be going too, since he hadn't run away screaming once the sun came up.

"Gimme everything you got," she said, then closed her eyes again and prayed for a miracle.

RYAN DUG A finger under his collar. It had to be at least two hundred degrees in this flowerbed. He and Mike had been standing on the small platform in the center of it since four o'clock sharp, and in the succeeding twenty minutes sweat had spouted from every pore.

To make matters worse, the constant trickling sound of the fountain had his bladder thinking inconvenient thoughts.

He'd warned Mike that punctuality had no place at a wedding, but Kate had said four o'clock and Mike was determined not to disappoint her.

Biting back *I told you so*, Ryan once again swiveled his head toward the bridal suite. Thank Jesus, the door opened. Out came Kate in a simple white dress with a long lacy veil that immediately swept out to the side like a flag in the breeze.

"My God," Mike breathed, "she's gorgeous."

"Gorgeous" was the word, all right. But Ryan wasn't looking at Kate.

Ellie had emerged right behind her. She paused, giving her friend the limelight. But to Ryan, Ellie was center stage.

She wore violet, a pretty sleeveless dress that was tight on top, as all good dresses should be, but with a flowy kind of skirt that fluttered in the sea breeze. Given his preference he'd like to see more leg—it hit in the middle of her calves—but he couldn't fault the dress's overall effect.

And he couldn't wait to peel it off of her.

Kate stepped to the railing so the photographer and his two assistants could set up some "candid" shots of the bride gazing out to sea. Then they drew Ellie into it, and Ryan's breath caught as she tossed her hair over her shoulder, the sunlight picking out strands of ginger and gold.

"How am I supposed to keep my hands off her?" Mike murmured.

"Good question," Ryan muttered.

He was still wondering about that fifteen long minutes later, when Ellie stood on the flowerbed platform beside him. He'd forgotten all about the heat, the sweat, and the shirt stuck to his back, because not touching her was taking every bit of his concentration.

Meanwhile, the photographer—André—bossed his

dogsbodies around, the beleaguered duo picking their way among the lilies, positioning a giant umbrella and a square of white canvas until at last he was satisfied.

"Ladies," he called out, "half a step forward, in front of the men."

Ellie took her place. Ry could see straight down her dress. Her matching pushup bra made mountains out of foothills—

André busted him. "Hey, big guy. Quit eye-groping her."

Ellie shot a blistering glance over her shoulder. He wolf-grinned.

Damn, he wanted her out of that dress. The bra, though, she could leave on. Panties too, since it was probably a matching set, most likely a thong—

"Eyes up here." André snapped his fingers.

They got it done eventually, and before he knew it he was standing beside Mike again, this time in the pretty white gazebo. Ellie was across from him beside Kate, tears in her eyes as the vows were exchanged.

This could be us. The words kept running through his mind. He tried to project them into Ellie's brain, and maybe she heard him, because her gaze flicked over to meet his. A fat tear broke loose and slipped down her cheek. His hand trembled with the need to wipe it away. To wipe away all of her tears, forever.

But no, forget that, it wasn't enough to wipe away her tears. He wanted to fight them before they ever had a chance to fall. To protect her from grief and injury, from the tiniest paper cut. From anything that might hurt her at all.

Another tear trembled on her lashes. He pushed his hands in his pockets to keep from reaching out—

A loud throat-clearing finally got his attention. "The rings . . ." the minister said, obviously not for the first time.

"Oh, shit," he blurted, which got a laugh from the half circle of guests assembled out on the lawn. It covered him while he dug around in his jacket for the box.

Passing it off to the minister, feeling like a douche for fumbling the only job he'd been given, he caught Ellie's gaze again. He grinned sheepishly, got a *you're such a doofus* grin in reply, and his heart swelled. His mood soared. *Hell yeah.* He'd embarrass himself a thousand times over, on purpose, if it made laughter from Ellie's tears.

When the ceremony ended at last and they'd processed out of the gazebo and stood mingling around the pool, Ellie approached him, tapping his arm with the folding fan she carried instead of a bouquet.

"Heatstroke?" she asked, spreading the fan and making a breeze.

"Must be. You should probably get me out of this tux."

Her lips tilted up in one corner. "Or I could push you into the pool."

"Only if you want to ruin that dress." He slid his

pinky under her shoulder strap, knuckled the soft skin beneath it. "Because you'd be getting wet right along with me.

"Or maybe I should say"—he leaned in, touched his lips to her ear—"you'd be getting wetter."

HEAT ROARED UP Ellie's neck, consuming her face. What was he, some kind of panther who could scent her pheromones?

Ry's cheek, already lightly bristled though he must have shaved an hour ago, scraped her jaw as he drew back, tingling her sensitized skin. His eyes, clear and bright though he'd slept no longer than she had, locked on to hers, scorching her with blue flame.

Damn him. It was pointless to pretend he wasn't getting to her. He knew her too well.

So she went with the truth. Sort of. "Guys in tuxes do it for me, what can I say?" She shrugged as if he was just any old guy in a tux.

"Lucky for me I'm the only guy here wearing one."

She raised a brow. "Mike's in a tux."

"Kate might have something to say if you jump her husband." His slow grin was like a hand sliding up under her skirt. "You should strip down the best man instead. I hear he's packing."

He covered her hand with his hot palm, which was when she noticed that somewhere along the line she'd flattened it on his chest. Now he slid it down toward his belt, apparently with every intention of continuing past it to show her exactly how much he was packing.

"Not here," she hissed, yanking her hand away.

"Then where? Because it's happening someplace." The look on his face said he wouldn't be denied.

She cast a furtive glance around. "We can't just leave. We're in the wedding party. They'll want more pictures."

His big hand slid around her waist and pulled her against him.

Yep, he was packing, all right. Fully loaded.

"We can make it fast," he said, like that was a big concession. "All we need is a closet. I'll do you standing up."

Oh Jesus, if she was wet before . . .

"They keep the towels in there." She tipped her head toward a shed with a louvered door on the other side of the pool.

"Let's go." He caught her hand and towed her through the crowd, nodding hello but stopping for no man.

Outside the door, she had second thoughts. "Someone could walk in."

"Then we better be quick," was his answer as he tugged her inside.

CHAPTER SIXTEEN

"WHERE WERE YOU?" Kate asked her, in full interrogation mode. "André wanted some shots up on the balcony while the sun was slanting across it."

"Fine, let's do it," Ellie said, smoothing her skirt. "Ry must be around here somewhere."

Kate's eyes narrowed. "He is *now*. But for some reason, nobody could find either of you for more than an hour. And believe me, *everyone* was looking."

Thank God none of them had thought to check the shed. Because, yeah, the stand-up quickie had devolved into an extended romp in a playpen full of towels.

The riot of dirty memories must've shown on her face, because Kate doubled down. "If you're going to eff up my wedding photos, you can at least share the details."

"What makes you think—"

Kate gave her a little shove toward the pool, just a few steps away. "You want to get wet, El?"

The wrong thing to say. Ellie's laugh exploded, loud enough that Ryan, ordering drinks at the bar, swung his head around. He met her eyes, and an irresistible smile broke out all over his face—lips, eyes, cheeks, the whole gorgeous package . . .

Package!

Ellie clutched her side and fended off Kate's next shove.

"Later," she told her friend. "After the honeymoon. It'll give you a reason to come back from Italy."

"That's mean." Kate pouted. "At least tell me where you did it. We checked your rooms, your cars . . ."

"Well, if you must know." Ellie flicked a glance toward the scene of the crime, then swished her shirt so a faint cloud of lint swirled around her ankles.

"But wasn't it hot in there?" the ever-practical Kate wanted to know.

"Oh, sweetie," Ellie said, smiling at Ryan as he made his way toward her, "you have no idea."

"Tanqueray and tonic for the lady," Ryan said, passing the dewy glass to Ellie.

"Thanks, lover." She dipped a finger in, sucked the gin off.

And didn't that go straight to his cock. Which was

pretty goddamn amazing considering the workout she'd just given it on Terrycloth Mountain.

Seriously, if nobody had filmed a porno in a towel shed yet, he had a few ideas—

A hand brushed at his shoulders. "My, my, look at all this lint," Kate said briskly. "It's almost like you were—oh, I don't know—*rolling around in beach towels.*"

He shot a startled glance at Ellie, who said, "She twisted my arm."

He shrugged. He didn't care who knew he was doing Ellie every chance he got.

In fact, his caveman liked the idea of publicly claiming her. Cinching her waist with one arm, he tugged her to his side, the twenty-first-century version of throwing her over his shoulder. To his delight, instead of shaking him off, she melted into him, hip to thigh. Even shifted her drink to her other hand so she could circle his waist too.

And that easily, they became two links in a chain, unbreakable as far as he was concerned. Warmth flooded his chest. Everything he wanted was literally within his grasp, and he knew without a doubt that he'd do whatever was necessary to hold on to it.

For starters, he'd move back to Boston. His old SWAT commander would welcome him back on the squad. Sure, it would suck to give up the promotion he'd busted ass for, the captain's bars he hadn't yet worn for a month. But it was worth it. Besides, he'd make captain in Boston in a couple of years.

All he needed was a nod from Ellie and he'd be on the phone giving LAPD his notice.

The problem was, he didn't think she was ready to commit to him out loud. He'd have to read the signals she was sending. Right now, for instance, her fingers dug around under his jacket, untucking his shirt, getting up under it, finding the super-sensitized skin between his ribs and his belt. Electricity sparked from the pads of her fingers; his nerve endings tingled.

He concentrated hard, his whole world shrinking down to her hand span, his every sense straining to decipher the message telegraphed by her fingertips. The secret code known only to Ellie. Small circles. Jagged lines. Fingernails scratching lightly. It was like Navaho code talk, impenetrable unless you'd been trained to decrypt it. What about this—a fingertip dipping under his waistband? Did it mean everything, or nothing?

And all the while she chatted endlessly with Kate, as if his entire future didn't teeter on the slightest pressure of her palm—

"Dude." Mike's voice startled Ry from his trance. Suddenly conscious that he'd been staring holes in the floor, he raised his head and focused on his brother, the groom.

"Hey, man," he said, dragging his mind back to business. "How's married life treating you?"

"You know how it is," Mike said with a meaningful smirk. "The single guys are having all the sex."

Ry smirked too because, yeah, since the wedding he'd definitely had more sex than the groom. A lot more.

"You missed a bunch of stuff," Mike informed him. "Champagne toast. Butler hors d'oeuvres."

"Nah, I got some of those spinach things—"

"Those were quiches," Kate interjected accusingly.

"Loved 'em," he said. "I couldn't stop eating 'em."

"He means that literally," Ellie said with a laugh. "He grabbed the whole tray from the waiter."

"I'm sure he worked up an appetite," Kate said, humor creeping into her voice.

"Must be the sea air." Ry tugged Ellie even closer. If he could, he'd wear her like clothes. Better yet, he'd get both of them out of their clothes . . .

"Don't even think about it," Kate-the-mind-reader growled. "You two aren't wriggling out of making toasts, and they better be good. If I'm not crying, keep trying."

"Got mine right here." Ellie whipped a crumpled paper out of her bra.

"Eww!" Kate reared back, palms up. "I don't wanna know how it got in that condition."

The folded scrap of paper had definitely seen some action. Ryan had a vague recollection of tunneling his way past it on his way down Ellie's dress.

"Good grief, Kate," Ellie sniffed, "marriage has turned you into a prude."

Ryan glanced at Mike. "Tough luck, dude. That explains your no-sex-since-the-wedding problem."

Kate eyed her new husband. "We've been married for all of an hour and a half!"

"Exactly," Mike said, spreading his palms as if she'd made his point for him. "An hour and a half in which every guy standing here has gotten laid but me."

Kate glowered. Mike let a smile creep across his face. Lifting her hand, he placed a kiss on her wrist, and she softened. He drew her against him, murmured into her ear, and like magic Kate melted and they were lost in their own world again.

Ellie regarded the whole episode with a jaundiced eye. "Well, that explains a lot. Seduction's in your DNA. You and Mike are both wired to get women into bed."

"I wish," Ry replied. "I've been working at it all weekend and I haven't gotten you into a bed yet."

Ellie rolled her eyes. "In this case, bed includes the towel shed. And the beach. And the floor."

"And the shower. I do good work in the shower." Ry had her wrapped in both arms now, one hand stroking the bare skin between her shoulders, the other splayed on her lower back, pressing her against the growing bulge in his pants.

"Think about it," he murmured. "Your legs around my waist. Your back against the tile. Steam rising up all around us." A hundred workdays they'd started like that, hot water hammering his back while he hammered her to the wall.

The heat in her eyes said she remembered it too. "We

can't disappear again," she murmured hoarsely. "Kate'll kill us."

"Mike's keeping her busy." Ry rubbed his nose in her hair, enjoyed her quivering exhale. "We'll be quick," he lied into her ear. "Just once for me, twice for you."

CHAPTER SEVENTEEN

BEFORE ELLIE COULD weaken—well, she was *already* weak—but before she totally folded, Kate caught wind of Ryan's shenanigans.

"Nuh uh." She squeezed Ellie's biceps in a vise. "*My* day. My *big* day."

Ellie should've felt relieved, but face it, she wanted Ry. Now. Later.

Always.

Whoa. That last part—the *always*—dropped like a bombshell out of the blue, exploding on contact, stopping her breath even as her pulse went wild.

She braced for panic to hit her. She should be fighting this, right? Shoving Ry into the pool and running for the hills?

Instead, she was grinning like an idiot.

Utterly disarmed, she gazed up into his face. God, how she'd missed his face. How she'd missed *him*.

As if he sensed the shift in her, his smile slowly widened into a come-and-get-me grin. She soaked it up, that grin of his. She'd take a bath in it if she could. Why, oh why, had she deprived herself of it for three long years? What foolishness could possibly justify that?

Regret gripped her heart, not hard enough to spoil the moment, but firmly enough to warn her not to blow this again. Ry was giving her another chance at *always*. He hadn't said it out loud, but every touch, every glance, held an invitation. *Come to me. Love me. Let me love you.*

Oh God, she wanted to. She'd wasted so much time! A thousand days and nights. For what? Because some hypothetical accident or terrorist or crazy ex-husband might snatch him away from her? Seriously, what were the odds? Lightning didn't strike twice. Hell, Jake's death practically inoculated her against losing another love. Right?

Ry moved his hand to her cheek, brushed his thumb over her lips. Maybe her heart was in her eyes, because his smile deepened. His fingers threaded her hair.

The world around them fuzzed out as all her attention honed in on him, touching her, loving her, thawing her frozen heart and filling it with love.

Nothing else matters, her brimming heart cried. Nothing could come between them now.

Nothing, that is, until Mike wrapped his big hand around Ry's shoulder and tugged him into a brotherly half hug. Reluctantly, Ellie emerged from her love-daze, tuning into Mike's voice just as he used his other hand to knock on Ry's skull. ". . . harder than that ball-peen hammer," he said. "Damn good thing, little brother, or instead of my wedding we'd be at your funeral today."

Funeral?

The word blasted into her brain like a tractor-trailer smashing through the front door, sudden and shocking, destroying everything. In an instant, her hopes fractured, her dreams fell in pieces, and her heart, her newly vulnerable heart, broke like glass.

Mike's lips continued to move as the skull-knock morphed into a noogie, but words were meaningless now. The guilty look on Ry's face killed any hope that it wasn't true.

Spinning away from his side, Ellie eluded his grasp and ran, dodging through the crowd, racing past the bar and the band, out onto the lawn. When her heels sank into the grass she kicked them off, fleeing blindly at first, then angling toward her room. She fumbled the key card out of her clutch and stabbed it into the slot, stumbling inside, slamming the door shut behind her.

Falling back against it, she gulped a breath. Sweat soaked her temples, her armpits.

Behind her, a palm slapped the door. "Open up, Ellie!"

She slid down till her butt hit the floor. "Jesus," she breathed. Calling for help. Begging for mercy.

Another slap. Desperation roughened Ry's voice. "Open the goddamn door."

"Go away," she said too softly. Then louder, "Go away, Ryan. I don't want to see you."

Silence descended.

She waited. Would he do it? Would he leave again, like he'd done the last time she asked him to?

A minute passed, the red LED numbers on the bedside clock rolling from 5:33 to 5:34, as she listened with every cell for the sound of footsteps walking away.

What she heard at last was a *shuss* as he slid down the other side of the door, then the thunk of his head, back to back with hers.

"Please, Ellie, don't do this."

Her hand trembled as she brought her fingers to her lips.

"Let me in, baby. I need to talk to you."

A thin thread of anger wove its way through the hurt. "A little late for that, don't you think?"

"I was gonna tell you—"

"When?"

"I was waiting—"

"For what? For the perfect moment to say 'by the way, Ellie, somebody tried to hammer my brains out through my butt'?"

"It wasn't like that."

"It doesn't matter what it was like." And wasn't that

the truth. Dead was dead. Didn't matter how it happened, it ended at the graveyard.

RY RIPPED OFF his stupid bow tie and balled it up in his fist. Mike was goddamn lucky it was his wedding day or he'd be on his way to the goddamn hospital right now to get his goddamn jaw relocated, and hopefully wired shut while they were at it.

Throwing the bow tie as far as he could—an unsatisfying three feet before it plopped onto the porch—Ry growled in frustration. How had everything gone to shit so fast?

It was all Mike's fault.

"Don't you dare blame Mike," came Ellie's voice through the door.

"Why not?" he grumbled. "He's an asshole."

"Sometimes," she allowed, "but not this time."

"He can't keep his mouth shut. Never could."

"Honesty's a good trait, Ry. You should try it." She sounded terrible. Heartbroken.

"I never lied to you, Ellie."

"A lie of omission is still a lie."

"I didn't *omit* it. I just hadn't gotten around to it yet." He would've. Eventually.

"Whatever, Ry. Just go."

"No." This time he wasn't leaving. "I'm coming home," he informed her. "I'm moving in next door. If you want to get rid of me, you'll have to move to California, because I'm back to stay."

For a long moment, she said nothing. Then, "I could use a change of scenery."

He ground his teeth. She'd do it, too. Ellie was stubborn like that.

He thunked his head against the door a few times. Maybe he could knock some sense into himself.

Then, as if things weren't bad enough already, Kate rounded the corner, Amelia and Julie on her heels. The grim set of their jaws said *You're toast, Ryan Murphy. Burnt toast.*

They pulled up in front of him, three red-hot Ferraris toeing the starting line, engines revving.

He thunked his head one more time.

"Careful," Kate snapped, "you'll dent the door with your thick skull."

"Look—" he began.

"No, *you* look." Julie glared down at him. "Mom—"

"—is right here," Ellie said, yanking the door open. "And I'm perfectly capable of ignoring thickheaded men on my own."

He peered up over his shoulder at the woman he loved, who was indeed ignoring him. "Please, Kate," she said, "don't let my stupid drama ruin your wedding. Go back to Mike. I just need a minute to regroup, then I'll come find you and we'll take embarrassing selfies for Facebook, okay?"

When Kate looked doubtful, Ellie added, "Don't worry about Ry. He was just leaving." She dropped her gaze to him. "Scat," she said, like he was a stray cat. Except she'd never chase away a stray cat.

He wouldn't let her chase him away either.

He pushed to his feet, clenching his fists at his sides to keep from reaching for her. "I'm not leaving till you hear me out," he said. "I'll sleep outside your door. I'll follow you home and sleep outside your door there too."

Ellie hissed in frustration. "You're an idiot."

She sounded angry, annoyed, and fed up. But gazing into her face, what he saw there was pain. A deep well of sadness in her eyes, a subtle tremor in her lips.

She was hurting, and he'd caused it.

"You're right. I'm an idiot," he said. He couldn't pretend otherwise. He'd known his close call would bother her, so he'd made up excuses to put off telling her. "I'm sorry," he said quietly, the two words that he should have led off with. "I was afraid to tell you. I was afraid of . . . this." He opened his palms to the chasm between them. "But it was selfish and dumb and sort of dishonest. And I'm sorry from the bottom of my heart."

As if they'd been waiting to hear the proper combination of contrition and humility, the Ferraris throttled back their engines to an approving murmur.

Ellie, on the other hand, stepped back inside and slammed the door.

CHAPTER EIGHTEEN

EVEN WITH HER fingers in her ears Ellie couldn't block out the commotion that ensued outside her door. Raised voices, everyone yakking at once, Ry digging in his heels about something.

Then, disconcertingly, silence.

It dragged on until curiosity got the best of her. She put her eye to the peephole. Her girls stood a few steps away, heads together, whispering. Kate had disappeared. There was no sign of Ry either. She stepped back, heart sinking. He'd given up on her again, left for good. Well, what did she expect? She'd ordered him to go.

A rap on the door brought her to the peephole again. Amelia and Julie, side by side like two shotgun barrels, locked and loaded.

Julie raised a fist to knock again, but Ellie whipped

the door open first. "We're not talking about it," she said. "Go away."

"Not happening," Julie said flatly, striding inside with Amelia right behind her. They shut the door and stood shoulder to shoulder in front of it, barring escape. "It's time for some real talk."

"Real talk?" Ellie crossed her arms. "This looks more like a firing squad."

Amelia fired first. "Do you wish you'd never met Dad?"

The shot ripped through Ellie's heart. She dropped her arms. "How could you ask such a thing? I loved your father!"

"That wasn't the question," Amelia pressed. "Do you wish you'd never met him?"

"She means," Julie added, "would your life be better if you'd never fallen in love with Dad? Would you be happier?"

Ellie drew back, shrinking into herself. How had she raised such hardhearted girls?

"Mom." Amelia came to her, curled an arm around her stiff shoulders. "We're not trying to hurt you."

"We're trying to make a point," Julie said. "You lost Dad, and it was terrible. We were too little to know what was up at the time, but for years afterward I remember going to his grave with you." Her voice wobbled. "You cried so hard every time. I can't imagine how much it hurt you to lose him."

"So you decided to bring it up today," Ellie said,

unshed tears making gravel of her voice. "The day my best friend gets married. The day I lose her too."

"You're not losing Kate," Amelia said firmly. "She's moving five minutes closer to you."

"But Mom." Julie took Ellie's hand. "You could lose Ryan today. If you chase him away again, he might not come back."

"Good," Ellie said, putting force into it. "He wants something he can't get from me."

"Love?"

Ellie blew out a frustrated sigh. "You girls. You think love's the answer to everything."

"Not everything," Amelia said. "But a lot. And it makes the other things bearable. Just think how much harder Dad's death would've been if you hadn't had us to love, and to love you."

"You don't understand," she said, and she hoped to God they never would. She wanted only happiness for them and their wonderful husbands.

"We understand that you closed your heart," Amelia said. "Not to us or your friends, but to the idea of a soul mate."

Ellie rolled her eyes. Amelia could be such a sap.

"But you still liked sex," Julie said, "and yeah, it's weird to talk about that, but we're letting it all hang out here, so deep breath everybody." She drew one of her own before continuing. "You still liked sex, so you tried having some superficial relationships, thinking you could keep things light—"

"It was working," Ellie cut in defensively.

"Until Ryan came along and you fell in love."

"You should've married him, Mom," Amelia said. "You should still marry him."

Ellie started to shove away from them, to get tough and tell them to mind their own business. But when she looked, really looked, into their beloved faces, so hopeful, so earnest, she couldn't do it. They only wanted what was best for her. How could she be mad about that?

Still, she needed to get them off her back.

So she tried reason and rationality instead. "I know Ry loves me," she said. There was no point denying it. "But marriage wouldn't be good for either one of us."

On her end, the risk of losing him to a crazed meth head, or a terrorist with a pressure cooker, or a school shooter with an AR-15 was intolerable. Ry might think he was invincible, but he was made of skin and bones and blood like everybody else was. Like Jake had been.

Answering the door to that kind of news about Ry would end her.

But there was no point in making that case to her daughters. They'd accuse her of catastrophizing, so she brought out her slam-dunk argument instead.

"Ry should have kids," she said quietly. "He'd be a great dad. The best. Depriving him of fatherhood would be the epitome of selfishness."

It was irrefutable, and yet her girls chuckled. "Nice try," Julie said, "but isn't that up to Ry?"

"Not everyone's cut out for parenthood," Amelia added. "It's a choice, not a requirement."

"Besides," Julie added, "he'll have me and Amelia."

Ellie huffed a startled laugh. "Honestly, Julie, can you see yourself calling him 'Dad'?"

Julie smiled, but she didn't laugh, not at all. "I can see myself calling him Ryan," she said gently, "just like I always have."

BECAUSE SHE INSISTED, Ry grudgingly followed Kate around the corner onto the hotel's front porch. The ocean view from there was stupendous, but he wasn't feeling it.

He was caught in a déjà vu nightmare. Three years ago, when he'd believed with everything in him that he and Ellie would be together forever, she'd dumped him. And he'd felt then exactly like he did now.

Hollowed out, sick to his stomach. Bereft.

Slumping along with his head down, he didn't realize Kate had stopped until he almost bumped into her. "Wake up," she snapped.

"Sorry." He fell back a step.

"That's not what I meant. I meant, wake the hell up about Ellie."

"Believe me, I wish this was just a bad dream."

Kate eyed him up and down, her laser beam gaze laying him open. Finally, she asked, "Why do you think Ellie keeps running away from you?"

"Because I'm younger—"

She chopped the air with her hand. "Thank God your brother isn't as dumb as you are."

He straightened up. "Mike never got above a C-plus in his life—"

"I'm talking about common sense. Being able to find your ass in the dark." She poked his chest. "Having a clue about human emotions."

"I know about emotions," he argued. "I know I love Ellie. And I know damn well she loves me."

Kate did a slow clap.

He dug deeper. "I even know she's worried about me dying."

"And do you know *why?*"

He reached back to his conversation with Julie and Amelia. "Because she equates love and husbands with death and heartbreak," he recited, pretty sure it was a direct quote.

"If it's that simple, why isn't she freaked out about her daughters' marriages? Or mine?"

He threw up his hands. "How should I know? You're the shrink, why don't *you* tell *me?*"

She cocked a brow. "Are you sure you want to go there? I charge double *during my own wedding.*"

That's right, he realized, she was standing here counseling him instead of dancing with her new husband. So he should probably shut up and listen.

He drew a deep breath, blew it out. "Sorry, Kate. If you've got any advice, I'd like to hear it."

"Okay." She seemed mollified. "But you don't really need my advice. You just need to think about what happened back there at the reception, the sequence of events. I know you have a *thick skull*, but . . ."

The lightbulb came on. The thick-skull clue helped.

"It's the job," he said.

"And it only took you three years to figure it out."

He scowled. "Somebody could've told me."

"Back then?" Kate waved that off. "What would you have done?"

"Quit," he said.

"Maybe eventually. But first you'd have told her she was being ridiculous, right?"

True, but he wasn't about to admit it now.

"Fights would've ensued," Kate went on, "and you'd have said things that hurt her." He started to object, but she held up a hand. "You wouldn't have meant to, but you would have, because you genuinely would've believed she was being silly." She touched his arm, making her point. "Out of blind love and ignorance, you would've minimized the most traumatic event of her life."

Anger welled up and he backed away, breaking contact. "If somebody had explained it to me, I could've been sensitive about it."

She tilted her head, raised her brows in a silent question. He crossed his arms, too mad to answer.

"Think back, Ry. The mayor had just hung a medal around your neck. The *Globe* kept you on the front page for a week. You thought you were invincible. Even if you knew how Ellie was feeling, you would've blown it off."

He wanted to deny it, but it rang awfully true.

Kate went on ruthlessly. "You would've argued that with how much you two loved each other, nothing else should matter. But I'm here to tell you that how much she loved you is *exactly* why it mattered."

"Okay," he said, only partly succeeding in pushing his anger aside, "let's say you thought you were doing the right thing, protecting her from an immature jerk who would've hurt her without meaning to. That was then. This is now. I don't think I'm invincible anymore. I understand I could die, and that my job probably makes it more likely, okay?"

"I don't know, Ry, *is* it okay?"

He wrestled with it. He loved being a cop, loved the hard training and adrenaline rush of SWAT. Giving it up . . . well, he'd never considered giving it up.

"Isn't there some way to convince her it's not as dangerous as she thinks?"

Kate studied him thoughtfully for a moment. "Why don't I tell you a story," she said, "and then we'll see if you can answer that question yourself."

"What kind of story?"

"The kind with an unhappy ending. It's about Ellie. Want to hear it?"

The last thing he wanted to hear was a sad story about Ellie. Just thinking about it tightened his chest. But if it meant understanding her better, he'd handle it.

Leaning her hip on the railing, Kate pointedly waited until he'd uncrossed his arms and propped his shoulders against the wall before beginning. "You already know that Ellie got married at seventeen," she said. "Jake was a few years older, and insanely crazy about her. She was head over heels too, completely wrapped up in him. You know what she's like, how she gives herself to people. To me, to her girls. Her students. You know how hard she loves."

He did. To be loved by Ellie was to feel like the center of the universe.

"Jake was a rookie, not even a year on the force when it happened, a hit-and-run while he was standing on the shoulder of Storrow Drive. I was with Ellie when they came to the door to deliver the god-awful news." Kate's voice caught. "If you'd seen her face, Ry. She just . . . crumpled."

Kate's eyes welled. "She thought they'd have years together, you know? And why wouldn't she? She was twenty, for Christ's sake. Not even legal to drink. Then the doorbell rings and, just like that, she's alone."

Ry tried to picture it and his heart squeezed: Ellie barely out of high school, full of joy and passion. Lavishing her love on the husband who adored her. Believing they'd go on like that forever.

"The girls were so young," Kate went on, swiping tears from her cheeks. "God, Amelia was in her playpen. Julie was toddling. She kept asking me why Mommy was crying." Kate shrugged helplessly. "Ellie was hardly more than a kid herself. Can you imagine what it did to her?"

He couldn't. Even now, with almost forty years of life experience to harden him, that kind of loss would shatter him. Imagining Ellie's tender twenty-year-old heart, her wide-eyed optimism, her total lack of preparedness when death came knocking at her door, he felt queasy.

Kate's voice broke. "She was defenseless, Ry. It absolutely crushed her."

CHAPTER NINETEEN

ELLIE HAD LEARNED to recognize Ry's mood by the volume and timbre of his knock.

This version was firm but civil, which likely meant he'd arrived at a momentous decision that he intended to explain to her in such a calm and rational manner that she couldn't help but instantly and unconditionally agree with him.

In other words, this was Reasonable Ry.

Standing right behind him would be Unreasonable Ry, ready to elbow him aside and barge into the room at the first inkling of resistance.

She rested her forehead against the door. She'd reached emotional redline. One more overwrought conversation with Ryan would push her over the edge—

"I quit the force," he called through the door.

She whipped it open. "You did *what*? Are you *crazy*?"

He leaned a hand on the frame, not pushing his way in, but she'd have to crush his fingers to close him out.

"I quit the force," he said calmly.

She stared hard at him. His blue eyes shone clear; he wasn't drunk. His face was California-suntanned, but not feverish.

"But . . . why?" she asked, stymied.

He took his hand from the door frame, shoved it in his pocket, and rocked slightly on the balls of his feet. "Maybe I'm brain damaged."

She snorted a laugh. "So what's new?"

He dropped his gaze, scuffed the ground. Terror seized her. Grabbing a lapel, she yanked him inside, where he stood gazing down at her solemnly. "Are you serious, Ry? Are you brain damaged?"

She searched his face, and he searched hers right back.

"No," he said at last. "I was kidding."

Relief swamped her, followed hard by annoyance. "Jerk," she said with a two-handed chest shove.

He fell back a step, looking sheepish. "Sorry. That was a dick move."

She let it go for now. "Did you really quit? Or were you kidding about that too?"

"I really quit."

Dear God, something terrible must have happened, even worse than getting hammered.

Needing space to breathe, she paced to the farthest

corner of the room, putting the bed between them. Her hands shook so she clasped them in front of her.

What had happened?

She wanted to know.

She didn't want to know.

She had to know. Because if she left it to her imagination, she'd never sleep again.

Facing him across the bed, she said quietly, "Tell me everything, Ry. And no more bullshit unless you really do want brain damage."

It occurred to Ry that he hadn't thought things all the way through. His entire plan came down to: resign from the LAPD; break the glad news to Ellie.

He'd assumed joyful tears and scorching makeup sex would follow, after which Ellie would agree to marry him and they'd live happily ever after.

When would he learn that nothing with Ellie ever went like he planned?

Quickly adjusting his thinking to sync up with reality, he met her anxious gaze and started from the beginning. "You know I've been on the job for twelve years, six of them with SWAT." She nodded. "Well, once I got to LA I started working a lot."

"You always worked a lot."

"More. Lots of overtime. It left me with less time to think. Less time to miss you."

Her gaze fell to the bed. Her fingers knotted more tightly.

"I got burned out," he said, matter-of-factly. "It happens to everybody, no one's immune. My mistake was that I didn't see it. I should've realized I wasn't at the top of my game and taken some downtime. Instead, I made a critical error that could've ended up a lot worse than it did."

His CO and the rest of the team had tried to convince him it was nobody's fault, but Ry wasn't buying it. He was team leader. He had to be smarter, faster, more careful than everybody else. And he was.

Until he wasn't. He must've missed something—a sound, a shadow, a movement of air that would have tipped him off—and as a consequence he'd nearly ended up on a slab. And it could've been worse—he could've lost a teammate. He never would've recovered from that.

Ellie had gone pale. "Tell me what happened," she said.

He told her.

When he finished she plopped down on the bed with her back to him, head bowed, shoulders shaking. He didn't know what to do. Should he go to her, hold her? He wanted to—it tore him up watching her cry alone. But everything about her posture said to stay back.

So he waited, helpless, fists clenched at his sides.

At last she wiped her eyes with her hem. Then she

stood and came around the bed to stand in front of him. In a quavering voice, she said, "You're so brave, Ry. I hate that about you."

He didn't know how to respond, and she didn't wait for him to find his words. "Why couldn't you be a regular guy? Like a plumber, or an electrician?"

That made him grin. "How about a ballplayer? I always wanted to play for the Sox."

"See what I mean? You'll never be happy with *ordinary*." Stepping closer, she smoothed the lapel she'd scrunched. "And that's exactly why you can't quit. Because you're extraordinary and you know it. If you don't get back on the horse, you'll doubt your nerve, and that'll eat you alive."

She knew him so well, and she was right; if he questioned his nerve, then self-doubt would kill him.

"I love you," she said. "I don't want you on the job, I don't. But you can't quit just because you think you screwed up." She slid her hand down his chest to pull his phone from his pocket. "Call back whoever you just called," she said, "and tell them you had too many tequila shots but now you've sobered up and you'll be back at work next month."

He plucked the phone from her fingers and slid it back in his pocket. Then he caught her hands and balanced them lightly in his own. "That's one of the many things I love about you," he said. "You want what's best for me, even when it's not what's best for you. But babe, I'm not scared to get back on the horse. Like I said, I'm burned out, is all. A couple weeks of vacation and I'll be five-by-five."

Her brow furrowed. "Then why quit?"

"Because I'm ready to come back to Boston. To come home."

"Okaaay." She nodded slowly. Then she straightened her shoulders, seemed to brace herself for bad news. "I guess that means you'll be going back to your old job. I'm sure your captain will be glad to have you back."

"As a matter of fact, I just talked to him." He released her hands, slid his palms up her arms to her shoulders. "He's a deputy superintendent now. A big cheese. He's got a wave of retirements coming up. Said he'd bring me in at my old rank."

She swallowed. Then she nodded. "Good. Good. Lieutenant, right?"

"Right. But not SWAT. Homicide. A detective unit."

Her eyes widened. She lifted them to his. "You mean, like, a desk job?"

He pretended to be offended. "It's not like detectives sit around all day," he said, conveniently forgetting that he'd frequently accused them of just that. "But they don't take a lot of fire either."

She seemed stunned. "Let me get this straight." She held up a hand, counted it off on her fingers. "You're coming back to Boston. You'll still be on the force. But you'll be solving homicides instead of throwing yourself in front of live ammunition."

"Yup."

She closed her hand and brought it to her chest. Then she bowed her head. He couldn't see her eyes, her expression. Had no idea what she was thinking. What if Kate was wrong about the SWAT thing? What if Ellie didn't want him anyway?

All he could do was hold his breath and worry, while glaciers melted into rivers, and nations were born and decayed, and every hair on his head turned grey.

When at last she brought her head up, he almost went to his knees, because tears of joy sheened her eyes; a half smile trembled on her lips.

With one slender finger, she tapped his chest lightly. "That's what you want?" she asked softly. "That's what you want in your heart?"

"That," he said gladly, "and you."

CHAPTER TWENTY

ELLIE AND RY scrapped their handwritten toasts and teamed up instead, an impromptu comic duo sharing hilarious stories about Kate and Mike. Their act was a hit, and by the time they wound down to the sentimental finale, even Kate was laughing through her tears.

After that, there was nothing left to do but dance the night away, together.

As evening fell, the band left the B-52s behind for Nat King Cole and Sinatra. On the dance floor couples swayed to "Stardust" under fairy lights that twinkled like stars.

Laying Ellie back over his arm in a shallow dip, Ry admired the graceful arch of her throat, the supple curve of her spine. She was strong as an oak, his Ellie, and flexible as a willow. She didn't need him to support her, but she trusted him to do it anyway. Pride swelled his chest. What better use of his strength than holding her safe as she danced through life at his side?

Pulling her close again, he soaked up her warmth as it seeped through his shirt to his skin, then deeper, all the way to his heart. For three years he'd somehow lived without her. An eternity that he prayed would end tonight.

Rubbing his cheek along her temple, he breathed in her lemony scent. "I bought your shampoo," he murmured, "when I was in LA. Used it once, then I had to throw it away."

She leaned back enough to look up at him, the lights playing over her face. "I slept with your Bruins shirt under my pillow for three months before I washed it and put it away."

He stroked her cheek. "I sweated a lot in that shirt."

"I had to change my pillowcase every night."

Pulling her in again, he buried his chuckle in her hair. Around them the reception wound on, but he was alone in his world with Ellie.

When the song ended, they linked hands and strolled along the grassy path to stand on the bluff. Before them, the indigo sky stretched to infinity. The crescent moon hung by a thread on the horizon, while Venus, in her glory, outshone the stars.

Below, waves threw themselves against the rocks then dissolved with a hiss, the foam gleaming faintly in the moonlight.

Ellie turned to him. "So I'm wondering," she said. "You're not quitting SWAT just for me, are you?"

He'd been waiting for her to get around to that. "At first I was," he said honestly, "but once it was done, it felt right. Not just for you, but for me too." He wasn't sure he could put it into words. "I used to love it, you know? But somewhere along the line I started using it like a drug. To charge me up. To numb me out." He shrugged. "I didn't realize it until today, till I quit."

"Hmm." She sounded skeptical. "That sounds like a rationalization. Like you decided to do it, then convinced yourself it was a good thing."

He cocked his head. "Seriously, El? You really think I'm that complicated?"

THAT SURPRISED A laugh out of her. "Good point," she admitted, relieved. She didn't want the full weight of his decision on her. Resentment was a slow-acting poison that ate away at love. No relationship could survive it, at least no relationship she wanted to be part of.

Ry brought her hand to his lips, dropped a kiss on her palm. "Don't get me wrong," he said. "There's nothing I wouldn't do for you, Ellie. No sacrifice I wouldn't make. But even if you walked away from me right now, I wouldn't change my mind about SWAT." He tucked her hand to his chest. "But please don't walk away."

Ellie gazed up into his face. Moonlight glinted in his eyes and cast his strong features in bas-relief. She reached up and lightly traced a fingertip down the bridge of his nose.

He sneezed.

She grinned. "I wondered if that would still work."

His eyes narrowed. "For somebody who hates to be tickled, you play a dangerous game."

Maybe. But her spidey-sense warned her that he was about to come out with something big—something life-changing—and the skittish part of her psyche couldn't help stalling.

But Ry wasn't having it. He captured her free hand before it could cause more mischief and laced his fingers through hers, binding her to him in the gentlest way.

"I've got a proposal for you," he said.

She tensed. This was it, he was about to pop the question. Panic tried to throttle her, but she forced herself to keep breathing. Her mind tore around in circles. What should she do? She wanted to be with him, no doubt, but *marriage*—

"I'm thinking about starting a team," he said.

Okay, not what she expected. "A team? What kind of team?"

"Well, you know how I said I always wanted to play for the Sox. That ship has sailed, so I thought, why not start my own team?" He squeezed her hands lightly. "Wanna play on it?"

Ah, so that was his game. Clever. "It depends," she said, narrowing her eyes. "What position do I play?"

"A winning team plays to its strengths." He released her hands to take ahold of her hips, tugging her closer. "So I'll pitch, you catch."

She hid a smile behind pursed lips. "Who calls the plays?"

"Team votes on the big stuff. General manager's in charge of the rest."

"Sounds like an important position."

"Critical. I've got my eye on a genius I'm trying to recruit for it."

She bit down on a grin. "Seems like your team needs a batter too. I know a guy who's got the equipment."

"Is he any good?"

"He gets around the bases."

"I'm gonna need more than that."

Ah, the bottomless male ego. "Well," she said cautiously, "I don't like to pile it on in case he ends up being a dud. But what I've seen is impressive. All-Star material, if you know what I mean."

He smiled smugly. "I guess we've got a team. Can I sign you?"

She held up a finger. "One question first." Searching his face, she wished the moonlight were brighter so she could read every nuance. "All joking aside, don't you want kids, Ry?"

"Grandkids'll do me fine," he said with no hesitation. "I can spoil 'em rotten and I'm not on the hook for college."

"Don't you want time to think about it?"

"I've been thinking about it for three years," he said. "I knew the answer then, and it hasn't changed."

He brought his hands up, cupped her face. "You're

the family I want, Ellie. You, and everyone who comes with you. The girls. Ray and Cody. Whatever kids they have, and whoever those kids marry. They're already mine in my heart. And you're at the center. You always have been. Always will be."

Cuffing his wrists, she felt his strength, his resolve. What had she done to deserve such a man's love? And how could she ever have been foolish enough to reject it?

"Okay, I'm in," she said.

"You're sure?" he asked. "I'm still nine years younger than you are."

She blinked a few times, then cocked her head. "Are you *trying* to make me change my mind?"

"I'm just sayin', there's no crying in baseball. No running off the field if the crowd turns nasty."

"Fine." She set a hand on her hip. "But the day some smart-ass asks if I'm your mother, I'm going at him."

"Never happen," he said confidently. "Now about that contract." Taking her right hand, he tapped the topaz ring on her middle finger. "This looks familiar."

"It should. You gave it to me for my birthday five years ago."

He wiggled it off, held it up to examine it in the moonlight. "I've got good taste," he declared. "But I'm afraid I'll have to take it back." His fist closed around it.

"Hey! I love that ring!"

"Then you'll be glad to hear I've got another one just like it." Passing it behind his back, he opened his other hand. "See? Looks the same, right?"

"Hmm. Some people might suspect that it *is* the same."

"People with a less discerning eye, sure. But any genius can see that this one goes on the *left* hand."

Taking hold of that hand, he paused a beat, gazing down into her eyes. "Ellie Marone," he said solemnly, "will you play on my team?"

His steady gaze held hers, his question and all it implied laid out plainly in his eyes. He was offering her the future and everything in it; love and heartache, joy and sadness. He'd share it all with her, the losses and the wins. All he asked was her promise that she'd do the same in return.

Well, of course she would. Why had she fought him so hard for so long? Why had she fought herself?

She didn't want to fight any longer.

What she wanted, really wanted, right down to the center of her soul, was to live every day with him, to curl up in his arms every night. To share all those highs and lows and, yes, old age and wrinkles.

She wanted the whole ball game. All nine innings.

"I will," she said as solemnly as he.

He breathed a sigh, and everything in him seemed to relax. A smile started to break out on his face, then disappeared when she abruptly closed her hand.

"Just one little condition," she said.

He elevated a brow.

"I want half ownership. Equal partners."

"Done," he said, and she opened her hand. He slid

the ring on her finger, then wrapped his arms around her in a hug so tight she lost her breath. His heartbeat thumped loud and fast under her ear, like he'd just run a race, or had the scare of a lifetime.

Pushing her hands up under the back of his jacket she found hot skin and damp cotton. Nobody watching would have guessed he was sweating it out. But she wasn't surprised. He played a cool game, with his SWAT nerves of steel. But he played for keeps.

And now, now at last he was hers to hold in the flesh. No more waking up aching and alone as dreams of him slipped away with the dawn. For the rest of their lives she'd have the real man to touch, to talk to, to laugh with.

"I love you," she murmured into the warmth of his chest.

"And I love you," he murmured back hoarsely. "With all my heart."

They clung to each other for a long time, to everything they'd almost lost. Finally Ry pulled back just enough to slide his palms up her arms. Moonlight glimmered in his eyes.

"Okay, babe," he said, "let's go play ball!."

Acknowledgments

BIG SHOUT-OUT TO my crit partners—Anna Bennett, Kari Cole, Ginny Frost and Autumn Jones Lake—fabulous authors, one and all!

Thanks for loving Ryan and Ellie and pushing me to write their story.

Keep reading for an excerpt of the first book
in the Save the Date series

The Wedding Favor

Available from Avon Books!

CHAPTER ONE

"THAT WOMAN" —TYRELL aimed his finger like a gun at the blonde across the hall— "is a bitch on wheels."

Angela set a calming hand on his arm. "That's why she's here, Ty. That's why they sent her."

He paced away from Angela, then back again, eyes locked on the object of his fury. She was talking on a cell phone, angled away from him so all he could see was her smooth French twist and the simple gold hoop in her right earlobe.

"She's got ice water in her veins," he muttered. "Or arsenic. Or whatever the hell they embalm people with."

"She's just doing her job. And in this case, it's a thankless one. They can't win."

Ty turned his roiling eyes on Angela. He would have started in—again—about hired-gun lawyers from New York City coming down to Texas thinking all they had to do was bullshit a bunch of good ole boys who'd never made it past eighth grade, but just then the clerk stepped out of the judge's chambers.

"Ms. Sanchez," she said to Angela. "Ms. Westin," to the blonde. "We have a verdict."

Across the hall, the blonde snapped her phone shut and dropped it into her purse, snatched her briefcase off the tile floor, and without looking at Angela or Ty, or anyone else for that matter, walked briskly through the massive oak doors and into the courtroom. Ty followed several paces behind, staring bullets in the back of her tailored navy suit.

Twenty minutes later they walked out again. A reporter from *Houston Tonight* stuck a microphone in Ty's face.

"The jury obviously believed you, Mr. Brown. Do you feel vindicated?"

I feel homicidal, he wanted to snarl. But the camera was rolling. "I'm just glad it's over," he said. "Jason Taylor dragged this out for seven years, trying to wear me down. He didn't."

He continued striding down the broad hallway, the reporter jogging alongside.

"Mr. Brown, the jury came back with every penny of the damages you asked for. What do you think that means?"

"It means they understood that all the money in the world won't raise the dead. But it can cause the living some serious pain."

"Taylor's due to be released next week. How do you feel knowing he'll be walking around a free man?"

Ty stopped abruptly. "While my wife's cold in the ground? How do you think I feel?" The man shrank back from Ty's hard stare, decided not to follow as Ty strode out through the courthouse doors.

Outside, Houston's rush hour was a glimpse inside the doors of hell. Scorching pavement, blaring horns. Eternal gridlock.

Ty didn't notice any of it. Angela caught up to him on the sidewalk, tugged his arm to slow him down. "Ty, I can't keep up in these heels."

"Sorry." He slowed to half speed. Even as pissed off as he was, Texas courtesy was ingrained.

Taking her bulging briefcase from her hand, he smiled down at her in a good imitation of his usual laid-back style. "Angie, honey," he drawled, "you could separate your shoulder lugging this thing around. And believe me, a separated shoulder's no joke."

"I'm sure you'd know about that." She slanted a look up from under thick black lashes, swept it over his own solid shoulders. Angling her slender body toward his, she tossed her wavy black hair and tightened her grip on his arm.

Ty got the message. The old breast-crushed-against-the-arm was just about the easiest signal to read.

And it came as no surprise. During their long days together preparing for trial, the cozy take- out dinners in her office as they went over his testimony, Angela had dropped plenty of hints. Given their circumstances, he hadn't encouraged her. But she was a beauty, and to be honest, he hadn't discouraged her either.

Now, high on adrenaline from a whopping verdict that would likely boost her to partner, she had "available" written all over her. At that very moment they were passing by the Alden Hotel. One nudge in that direction and she'd race him to the door. Five minutes later he'd be balls deep, blotting out the memories he'd relived on the witness stand that morning. Memories of Lissa torn and broken, pleading with him to let her go, let her die. Let her leave him behind to somehow keep living with-out her.

Angela's steps slowed. He was tempted, sorely tempted. But he couldn't do it. For six months Angela had been his rock. It would be shameful and ugly to use her this afternoon, then drop her tonight.

Because drop her, he would. She'd seen too deep inside, and like the legions preceding her, she'd found the hurt there and was all geared up to fix it. He couldn't be fixed. He didn't want to be fixed. He just wanted to fuck and forget. And she wasn't the girl for that. Fortunately, he had the perfect excuse to ditch her.

"Angie, honey." His drawl was deep and rich even when he wasn't using it to soften a blow. Now it flowed like molasses. "I can't ever thank you enough for all you did for me. You're the best lawyer in Houston and I'm gonna take out a full- page ad in the paper to say so."

She leaned into him. "We make a good team, Ty."

Sultry-eyed, she tipped her head toward the Marriott. "Let's go inside. You can . . . buy me a drink."

His voice dripped with regret, not all of it feigned. "I wish I could, sugar. But I've got a plane to catch."

She stopped on a dime. "A *plane*? Where're you going?"

"Paris. I've got a wedding."

"But Paris is just a puddle-jump from here! Can't you go tomorrow?"

"France, honey. Paris, France." He flicked a glance at the revolving clock on the corner, then looked down into her eyes. "My flight's at eight, so I gotta get. Let me find you a cab."

Dropping his arm, she tossed her hair again, defiant this time. "Don't bother. My car's back at the court-house." Snatching her briefcase from him, she checked her watch. "Gotta run, I have a date." She turned to go.

And then her bravado failed her. Looking over her shoulder, she smiled uncertainly. "Maybe we can cel-ebrate when you get back?"

Ty smiled too, because it was easier. "I'll call you." Guilt pricked him for leaving the wrong impression, but Jesus, he was itching to get away from her, from every-one, and lick his wounds. And he really did have a plane to catch.

Figuring it would be faster than finding a rush-hour cab, he walked the six blocks to his building, working up the kind of sweat a man only gets wearing a suit. He ignored the elevator, loped up the five flights of stairs—why not, he was soaked anyway—unlocked his apartment, and thanked God out loud when he hit the air-conditioning.

The apartment wasn't home—that would be his ranch—just a sublet, a place to crash during the run-up to the trial. Sparsely furnished and painted a dreary off-white, it had suited his bleak and brooding mood.

And it had one appliance he was looking forward to using right away. Striding straight to the kitchen, he peeled off the suit parts he was still wearing—shirt, pants, socks— and balled them up with the jacket and tie. Then he stuffed the whole wad in the trash compactor and switched it on, the first satisfaction he'd had all day.

The clock on the stove said he was running late, but he couldn't face fourteen hours on a plane without a shower, so he took one anyway. And of course he hadn't packed yet.

He hated to rush, it went against his nature, but he moved faster than he usually did. Even so, what with the traffic, by the time he parked his truck and went through all the rigmarole to get to his terminal, the plane had already boarded and they were preparing to detach the Jetway.

Though he was in no frame of mind for it, he forced himself to dazzle and cajole the pretty girl at the gate into letting him pass, then settled back into his black mood as he walked down the Jetway. Well, at least he wouldn't be squished into coach with his knees up his nose all the way to Paris. He'd sprung for first class and he intended to make the most of it. Starting with a double shot of Jack Daniel's.

"Tyrell Brown, can't you move any faster than that? I got a planeful of people waiting on you."

Despite his misery, he broke out in a grin at the silver-haired woman glaring at him from the airplane door. "Loretta, honey, you working this flight? How'd I get so lucky?"

She rolled her eyes. "Spare me the sweet talk and move your ass." She waved away the ticket he held out. "I don't need that. There's only one seat left on the whole dang airplane. Why it has to be in my section, I'll be asking the good Lord next Sunday."

He dropped a kiss on her cheek. She swatted his arm. "Don't make me tell your mama on you." She gave him a little shove down the aisle. "I talked to her just last week and she said you haven't called her in a month. What kind of ungrateful boy are you, anyway? After she gave you the best years of her life."

Loretta was his mama's best friend, and she was like family. She'd been needling him since he was a toddler, and was one of the few people immune to his charm. She pointed at the only empty seat. "Sit your butt down and buckle up so we can get this bird in the air."

Ty had reserved the window seat, but it was already taken, leaving him the aisle. He might have objected if the occupant hadn't been a woman. But again, Texas courtesy required him to suck it up, so he did, keeping one eye on her as he stuffed his bag in the overhead.

She was leaning forward, rummaging in the carry-on between her feet, and hadn't seen him yet, which gave him a chance to check her out.

Dressed for travel in a sleek black tank top and yoga pants, she was slender, about five-foot-six, a hundred and twenty pounds, if he was any judge. Her arms and shoulders were tanned and toned as an athlete's, and her long blond hair was perfectly straight, falling forward like a curtain around a face that he was starting to hope lived up to the rest of her.

Things are looking up, he thought. *Maybe this won't be one of the worst days of my life after all.*

Then she looked up at him. The bitch on wheels.

He took it like a fist in the face, spun on his heel, and ran smack into Loretta.

"For God's sake, Ty, what's wrong with you!"

"I need a different seat."

"Why?"

"Who cares why. I just do." He slewed a look around the first-class cabin. "Switch me with somebody."

She set her fists on her hips, and in a low but deadly voice, said, "No, I will not switch you. These folks are all in pairs and they're settled in, looking forward to their dinner and a good night's sleep, which is why they're paying through the nose for first class. I'm not asking them to move. And neither are you."

It *would* be Loretta, the only person on earth he couldn't sweet-talk. "Then switch me with someone from coach."

Now she crossed her arms. "You don't want me to do that."

"Yes I do."

"No you don't and I'll tell you why. Because it's a weird request. And when a passenger makes a weird request, I'm obliged to report it to the captain. The captain's obliged to report it to the tower. The tower notifies the marshals, and next thing you know, you're bent over with a finger up your butt checking for C–4." She cocked her head to one side. "Now, do you really want that?"

He really didn't. "Sheeee-iiiit," he squeezed out between his teeth. He looked over his shoulder at the bitch on wheels. She had her nose in a book, ignoring him.

Fourteen hours was a long time to sit next to someone you wanted to strangle. But it was that or get off the plane, and he couldn't miss the wedding.

He cast a last bitter look at Loretta. "I want a Jack Daniel's every fifteen minutes till I pass out. You keep 'em coming, you hear?"

Keep reading for a sneak peek
at Cara Connelly's next novel in
the Save the Date series

The Wedding Dance

Available soon from Avon Impulse!

CHAPTER ONE

A SHADOW FELL across the floor, long and dark.

Mari glanced over her shoulder. In the doorway a tall, broad man stood silhouetted against the brilliant Italian sun.

She'd left her studio door open to the warm September air on the off chance potential students might wander in. She'd assumed they'd run more to six-year-old ballerina wannabes than to strapping adult males, but with her grand opening just two weeks away she wasn't choosy.

Releasing the barre, she plucked a towel from the back of a chair. "Can I help you?" she asked, hoping English would do. Ten years in Portofino and she still hadn't mastered Italian.

The adult male in question stepped over the threshold, then paused, tucking his hands into his pockets. "I sure hope so," he said, his deep baritone unmistakably

American, appealingly infused with a slight Western twang.

It rang a bell, that voice, but she couldn't quite place it. Dabbing her cheeks, she looked closer. His features were lost against the bright light behind him, but she could make out the shape of his body just fine, and there was nothing not to like. He was seriously built, standing a few inches taller than her own six feet and packing enough lean muscle into his tight T-shirt and jeans to wake her girl parts from their long winter nap.

"If you're looking for lessons," she said, "I'll be glad to take your name and contact info. Classes begin two weeks from Saturday."

"Two weeks?" He sounded disappointed. So was she, even more so as he moved into the room, all masculine grace and chained power, and began a slow prowl around the perimeter. He'd be a natural dancer, she thought, a pleasure to work with.

A very desirable student in every way.

His roaming took him to the farthest corner of the bare room, the deepest shadows, where he turned to face her. "What if—" he began, then did a double take and whipped off his sunglasses. "Well fuck me," he blurted, "if it's not Maribelle Monroe."

She froze, shocked out of her socks. "Oh my God." A mere whisper, because the air had been sucked out of the room.

Before her stood Cash Sullivan, Hollywood hotshot, as mega as a movie star could get.

He spread his hands, let out a long whistle. "Mari, honey, you just might be the last person I expected to find here. Hell, what's it been? Five years?"

"Ten." A full decade. And not nearly long enough.

"Damn. Time fucking flies, doesn't it?" The concept must have amused him, because his legendary laughter spilled out. Mari tried not to get any of it on her, but it saturated the room, a rich, sensual rumble irresistible to femalekind. So seductive, in fact, that urban legend proclaimed he'd once roused a woman from a coma with it.

Needless to say, no one ever asked why he'd been laughing it up at the patient's bedside. Who really cared? Like everything else Cash Sullivan did, it was accepted without question. Acclaimed and glorified, exaggerated and hyperbolized. And then it was retweeted ten thousand times to his legions of fans around the globe, on the space station, and in a galaxy far, far away.

He was categorically and universally adored.

Who, *People Magazine* had once asked, rhetorically, didn't love Cash Sullivan?

Maribelle Monroe, that's who.

"Out," she said. "Get out."

He quit laughing and reared back like she'd slapped him. "Wait, what?"

"I said get out." She stabbed a finger at the door.

His hands dropped to his sides. "For real?"

She marched to the open door and did a right-this-way arm sweep toward the sidewalk.

"But—"

"No buts. No talking, no laughing, no thank you. Just out."

He drooped like a puppy left at the pound. "You're not glad to see me?"

She cupped a hand to her ear. "That noise you just made? That's called talking. We're not doing that." Another arm sweep.

He took an uncertain step toward the door, almost as if the earth had begun quaking under his heels and he was afraid to put a foot wrong and vanish into a crevasse.

If only.

More likely, though, he was in shock. He'd probably never been kicked out of anyplace in his life. Mari knew for a fact that he could tear up a bar in a brawl, then shotgun beers with the owner while the poor suckers he'd flattened got hauled off to jail or the hospital. Either way, he was immune because, hey, who'd complain about having their skull cracked by the awesome Cash Sullivan?

He was so grossly beloved that even his exes adored him. The sweetest guy, they claimed. A true gentleman, the most generous man alive, blah blah. Well, why wouldn't they worship him? With the pull of a string he could land them any role they wanted, and frequently did. It was his classic breakup gift, guaranteed to leave them smiling.

No matter who else got trampled in the process.

That he was cheerfully oblivious to the destruction he left in his wake excused none of it. It was simply a testament to an ego so bloated, a psyche so self-centered, a personality so one-dimensional—

He took another hesitant step. It brought him out of the shadows and into the light, giving Mari her first good look at him. She gasped.

Gone was the sandy-haired surfer dude with the ocean-blue eyes, whose boyish good looks made him a poster boy for California living. Instead she was eye to eye with a biker straight off *Sons of Anarchy*, a black-haired, leather-vested menace to society with a three-day beard, two full sleeves of ink, and a pair of battered black boots built for neck stomping.

He took her gasp as an invitation to start blabbing again.

"I'm incognito," he said. "You know, in disguise."

"I know what incognito means," she snapped. "It just startled me, is all. I was expecting your usual stars and stripes and apple pie."

"Still here," he said with a grin designed to melt hearts and panties and the last of the glaciers.

She puckered up sourly. Two entire successful movie franchises had been built on Cash Sullivan's unnerving ability to morph from fair-haired golden boy to squinty-eyed stone killer in the space of a heartbeat. Now, with a flash of his grin he'd just pulled the same act on her in reverse, and she felt manipulated. Foolish. And deeply annoyed.

Naturally, he was insensible to her displeasure. Instead

of taking the hint and slinking out the door, he assumed she was dying to hear details.

"You're probably thinking it's a lot of work," he said, "and you're not wrong. These fake tats alone take two guys a whole day." He rotated his arms, sure she'd be longing for a closer look. And she had to admit they were worth admiring. Not the tats, she couldn't care less about those. But the muscles? Well, whoever was training him these days deserved an Oscar for best scenery.

"But the rest of it's cake," he went on. "I mean, I don't love dyeing my hair, and this itches like a bitch"—he scrubbed his beard—"but it's worth it to walk around like a normal guy for a while."

A normal guy. She breathed slowly through her nose. A normal guy couldn't wave a hand and make another actor's career skyrocket—or crash and burn.

"Damn," he said with a dazed shake of his head, "I still can't believe it's you. You look as amazing as ever. Always the prettiest girl at the party." His brow furrowed. "Why'd you bail?"

As if she'd ever tell *him*, the guy who'd tanked her career as easily and unconsciously as he'd have swatted a fly. "Why does anyone?" she said instead.

He scratched his head. "You know, I'm not sure."

Of course not. His puny mind couldn't comprehend what it might be like for the multitudes who never attained stratospheric stardom. Who survived for years on character roles and bit parts until they aged out of Hollywood.

Or whose careers never got off the ground at all because they lost their big break to one of Cash Sullivan's castoffs three days before shooting began.

WHAT THE HELL, Cash wondered, had he done to piss off Maribelle Monroe so bad that she carried a ten-year grudge? He couldn't imagine. Hell, he'd barely said two words to her in Hollywood. Mostly he'd admired her from afar, the untouchable ice princess, too beautiful to be mere flesh and blood.

But based on the way she was glaring at him—like she wished he'd spontaneously combust—he must've fucked up her life in some major way.

At least he'd managed to get her talking. Maybe if he kept the convo going she'd open up to him. He was a good listener. All his girlfriends told him so. Which was probably why they felt free to elaborate on his many failings while they were at it.

But Maribelle wasn't an old girlfriend, so he couldn't fathom how he'd offended her. He'd sure like to know so he could apologize, but with her hand on the doorknob and a mulish look on her face, she didn't seem inclined to enlighten him.

So he rubbed his stubble, a move that usually distracted women enough so they dropped the frying pan they'd been aiming at his head.

It caught Maribelle's eye too, and though it wasn't likely to hold her attention for long, it bought him crucial seconds to get the bearings he'd lost the moment he recognized her. Finding her here, about as far away from Hollywood as a person could get, had not only blindsided him but complicated his whole game plan, which had been shaky from the start.

All things considered, he'd just as soon take her up on her invitation to GTFO, but since he needed her help he'd have to hunt for common ground instead.

A glance around the room held little promise—a bare-bones dance studio with polished wood floor, barre along one wall, mirrors lining two others. Framed prints leaned against the fourth wall waiting to be hung, and a single folding chair held a towel, a black gym bag, and a grey hoodie.

He stole another glance at Maribelle too, not long enough to qualify as an eye-grope, but sufficient to appreciate her tall, willowy shape and waist-length white-blond hair, currently tied back with a silk scarf the same shade of pink as her leotard.

In LA they'd called her breathtaking. Unearthly. Ethereal.

She was all of that now, and more.

Unfortunately, *more* included less tolerant of pushy A-listers. Back then she'd chatted politely, if distantly, when he'd finally gotten up the balls to approach her. Her current expression had his balls ducking for cover.

He shoved his hands deeper into his pockets, as if it would help, and tipped his head toward the stacked prints. "I'm nobody's notion of a handyman," he said, "but I can hammer a nail."

That got a raised brow and an amused, "That could be fun to watch."

Hoping he'd mash his thumb, no doubt. Well, he had news for her. Growing up in Oklahoma he'd strung miles of barbwire with only a handful of notable injuries.

She seemed to consider it for a moment, then released the doorknob with a shrug. "Hardware store's two blocks down on your right. Bring me the receipt and I'll reimburse you."

Excellent! Common ground found. "Be right back," he said, and darted out the door.

It slammed behind him. The dead bolt snicked into place.

What the fuck? She'd outsmarted him and it stung like a bee.

Well, this wasn't over.

Ten minutes later he was back with a hammer and a bagful of nails. He rapped on the door.

"Get lost, dickhead," she called through it.

"I bought your stuff," he called back. "Got the receipt right here."

A snort issued from inside. "Slide it under the door."

"It's on my phone." A lie he justified by taking a quick photo of it before shoving it deep in his pocket.

Annoyed silence. Then, "What did you make on

your last film? Twenty mil? How can you be such a cheapskate?"

"I'm not the one reneging on my debts," he pointed out.

More annoyed silence, then the door swung open. She was already stalking toward her bag when he stepped over the threshold.

"Might as well let me help," he said to her back. "It's a two-man job. One to hold it up and move it around while the other decides where it should go."

She smirked at him over her shoulder. "I'm the brains and you're the brawn?"

"What do you think?" He popped his biceps.

She snickered, not the reaction he was used to. Why was she hating on him? Sure, he could name some women from his past who'd gladly greet him at the door with a shotgun, but with Mari he shared no history. No sex, no romance, no film credits. None of the things that normally pissed women off.

Still, he couldn't rule out having done something dumb back in the days when stardom was shiny and new, and throwing his weight around had given him the illusion of power. He'd been slow to understand he was confusing favors with clout. Favors could evaporate overnight. One box office failure and the folks with the real power would've left him out in the cold.

He was one of them now, and he'd earned it the hard way. He'd busted his ass and still did, producing, script-doctoring, occasionally directing, always starring in, frequently financing, and consistently making millions on, every one of his films.

"Whatever it takes," was his motto, on screen and off. He'd built his brand around it: all-American hero, ready, willing, and absolutely capable of doing everything required to defeat the forces of evil, be they foreign, domestic, alien, zombie, or his own inner demons. He took them all down in the end, Cash-style.

Now, though, real life had thrown him a curve he wasn't equipped to deal with, and in its circuitous way it had brought him here, to the only dance studio in Portofino.

Cash hadn't waltzed through the door by chance. He'd come because he needed to learn dancing. It was the last skill he'd ever expected to need; the only one he'd ever dreaded tackling.

Talk about your inner demons.

Thanks, Pop, for fucking me up so bad.

My pleasure, son. Here, have some PTSD with your PBJ, then get your pansy ass outside and practice your fucking drills. And don't you ever forget what I told you, boy: Fairies dance; real men play football.

Cash hadn't forgotten. Sheer repetition had imprinted it, and Pop's object lessons had ground it in so deep that even though Cash had long ago rejected the rest of the old man's homophobic, misogynistic, warped and perverted bullshit, he'd never brought himself to step onto a dance floor, or even tap his foot to the radio.

So he was starting from zero, and he'd procrastinated himself into a corner. Dread it or not, he needed to get some moves under his belt, and fast. Since Mari's studio was the only game in town, he'd have to convince her to set aside her grudge.

Whatever it takes, he thought, and crossed the room to lift a print off the stack. "Tell me where you want it."

"A LITTLE TO the left," Mari said. "Another inch. Higher." She tilted her head. Motioned to the right. Then, "Hmm, no, bring it back to the center."

Fifteen minutes they'd been at it and they were still on Baryshnikov. Cash was sweating freely. Mari was trying not to laugh.

She laid a finger along her jaw. "You know, I don't think Mikhail's gonna work there after all. Let's try a different one."

Stoically, Cash leaned Mikhail against the wall, picked up Margot Fonteyn.

Mari tapped her chin. "A little to the left."

Ten minutes later Cash finally rebelled. "Why don't we switch positions for a while?" he said, lowering Margot to the floor. "I guarantee it'll help you make up your mind."

She feigned surprise. "Don't tell me all those muscles are just for show."

"Let's see you hold those frames up all morning." He stomped across the room to rifle her bag.

"Hey!" She charged over and yanked it out of his hands.

"You can't work me like a rented mule if I die of thirst," he crabbed.

"You could've asked," she crabbed back at him. She dug out a spare water bottle and he snatched it from her. "It's that leather vest," she said while he chugged. "That's why you're so hot."

He wiped his lips with the back of his hand. "Finally," he sneered, "the ice princess admits I'm hot."

"That's not what I meant and you know it." She dropped her bag on the chair and strode away from him because, in fact, he *was* hot. Hot, as in sweating out pheromones so potent that even hating him with all her might couldn't neutralize them.

When she'd reached a safe distance, she said with fake regret, "We better call this off. What if you strain a tendon or break a fingernail? You could be laid up for weeks."

He capped the water bottle and dropped it back into her bag.

Then he stalked toward her, grim-faced.

She backed up a step.

He stopped an arm's-length in front of her and she found herself caught in an eye-lock, his sapphire irises glinting like sunlight off a gun barrel.

She gulped. Damn it, his pheromones really packed a punch.

"So," he said, lips twisting in a smirk, "you think I'm hot."

"Uh, that's not exactly what I said—"

"Either way." He shrugged off his vest. It hit the floor with a thump.

"I'm not sure that's really gonna help—"

"Then how about this?" He peeled off his T-shirt.

"Oh Jesus!" She threw up a hand to block the view. "Save it for Instagram."

"Been following me, have you?"

"Please. You've got nothing I want to see."

When he didn't snap out a comeback she peeked through her fingers. He'd looped his T-shirt around his neck and crossed his arms over his pecs.

Very nice, those pecs. No danger of straining one of those bad boys by hefting a few prints. His shoulders were probably safe too, being so broad and all.

She'd already had ample exposure to his arms, but at this range she got a close-up of the tats. They looked totally legit and, she had to admit, badass as hell. Framed against the bronzed background of his chest, they were art—

He chuckled and her gaze flew to his face. The jerk winked at her.

She dropped her hand. "Gross."

He grinned but didn't call her out any further. "Let's hang some prints, Princess. It's almost lunchtime. You don't want to see me hangry."

He slid the shirt off his neck, dropped it on top of the vest, and headed for Margot, giving Mari a load of his back. It was, she knew, a deliberate provocation, a lure, but it was also a perfect and powerful V. Two cords of muscle bracketed his spine. His lats spread out like compact wings. His waist was as taut as Baryshnikov's.

He bent down for the print. Straightened up and raised it above his head. Extended his arms and lowered them a few times.

She licked her lips.

"I saw that," he said, startling her.

Silently cursing the mirror-lined walls, she pointed at a spot she'd rejected at least twice before. "Hang it there."

"You're sure? Cuz I was thinking—"

"Don't think," she cut in. "Overtaxing your muscles is one thing. But brain damage, well, I'd never forgive myself."

He grinned, eyes twinkling. "You're funny, Princess. Who knew?"

"What's that supposed to mean?"

"Just that I've never seen you laugh. I'm no comedian, but I can get a laugh out of most folks. Pretty sure I've never even seen you smile."

"Maybe I don't find you amusing."

"That's exactly my point. *You* don't find me amusing."

"So *I* must be the one with the problem?"

"Well, not to put too fine a point on it, but yeah."

Holding out the hammer—handle first so she wouldn't be tempted to bash him with it—she said lightly, "I warned you about breaking your brain. Now you've gone and done it."

He took the hammer with a chuckle. When he finished pounding the nail—and looking damn good doing it—she checked her watch. "Gee, you were right about lunchtime. Buh bye now."

"No 'thanks, Cash, I couldn't have done it without you'?"

"Please. I totally could've done it without you."

He gave her a long look, during which she gave him one back.

Neither of them blinked. Neither of them smiled.

He tried to break her by making a production out of finger-combing his hair, which called for spreading his elbows wide to display the full wonder of his torso. Not coincidentally, it also allowed his jeans to slip down a few critical inches, exposing the flat tawny plane of his belly and stopping *juuuust* short of the line separating PG-13 from R.

She kept her head, following the happy trail with peripheral vision only, and countered by reaching back to loosen the scarf holding her hair. She let the pink silk slither to the floor at his feet, then coolly slid an arm under her hair and swept it forward over one shoulder, where it cascaded to her waist in a shining gold waterfall.

He didn't blink, not really, but his eyelids flickered. So she tossed her head a little to set the strands shimmering. His lips flattened in response, but she could practically see him double down. It would take more than a yard of blond hair to crack him—

Then his phone went off, "Can't Touch This" blaring from his pocket, and they were so into their stare-off, so focused, so intense, that they both leapt like cats, straight up and down.

It was acutely embarrassing.

Cash recovered first. "I gotta get that," he said, and while he dug out his phone Mari slunk back to her gym bag to slug half a bottle of water and ask herself how she'd gotten sucked into a staring match with Cash Sullivan anyway.

Even worse, how had she spent the whole morning with him?

Turning her back, she tried to ignore him. But since *sotto voce* wasn't in his vocabulary, she couldn't help overhearing his side of the conversation. "Gimme an hour," he said. "Can you hold out that long?"

She rolled her eyes. Seriously? Did the guy believe his own hype?

A pause followed while the pathetic female on the other end of the call undoubtedly fondled his ego. Then his laugh rolled out, and Jesus, it was loud. Wake a coma patient? He could wake the dead with that thing.

In the mirror she saw him slip the phone into his pocket, then tug his shirt over his head. He caught her watching, of course, but she gave him no time to gloat, hitching her thumb toward the door. "Don't let it hit you on the way out."

In response, the contrary bastard grinned, shrugging into his vest as he swaggered her way.

She eyed him resentfully as he came. He really could pass for a biker. Except for his grin, that is. No biker could possibly have lips as full, or teeth as perfectly imperfect, with just one crooked incisor to prove he was human and not the handiwork of some mad—female—scientist bent on creating the ideal male specimen.

He walked around her to retrieve his water bottle from her bag. She tapped her foot while he drained it, then held out her hand. "Gimme."

"No trash can?"

"Not yet." She snatched it from him. "I told you, I'm not open for another two weeks."

He scratched his chin thoughtfully. Shuffled his feet, checked his watch.

For God's sake, what the hell was his problem? "Look, do you need directions or something? Do you even know where you . . ." She trailed off as a belated thought struck her. "Wait a second. What made you walk in here in the first place?" Her studio was hardly a tourist attraction.

He hesitated, then exhaled a sigh. "Truth is, I need to learn . . ." He drew circles in the air with his hands.

"Is that supposed to be dancing?"

He pointed at her. "Exactly."

She snorted a laugh. "You came here to learn dancing? From me?"

"From whoever," he said. "I didn't know it would be you."

"Well tough luck," she said, crossing her arms, "because it *is* me. And the answer is no."

"BUT WHY?" CASH glanced around the empty room. "You're not doing anything else."

"As a matter of fact," she said sharply, "I'm doing a lot, or I was before you screwed up my whole morning." She ticked it off on her fingers. "Cleaning, painting, polishing, promotion—"

"So hire somebody for the grunt work. I'll pay for it. Then you can devote yourself entirely to me."

She made a choking sound and her cheeks sprouted red flags. "Cash Sullivan, you are the most presumptuous, self-centered, egotistical—"

"—jackass you've ever met. Yeah, yeah, I know. I get that you don't like me. Care to tell me why?"

She sniffed. "In order to dislike you I'd have to care about you. I don't."

"Uh-huh." Well, she'd tell him when she was ready. They always did. For now, he said, "Then let's cut to the chase. Twenty thousand for two weeks of private lessons."

Her mouth fell open. A very gratifying response.

She stared at him as long seconds ticked by. Then her ice-blue eyes narrowed. "Dollars or euros?"

"Your call."

She went silent, and he could practically hear her running the numbers in her head, balancing the books, weighing her options. Which was exactly what he wanted her to do. He'd calculated his offer carefully; too large to dismiss out of hand, but not so outrageously disproportionate that she'd sense his desperation and reject it out of spite.

As her silence dragged on he refrained from checking his watch or signaling the slightest impatience. He'd be late for lunch at this rate, but the negotiations had reached a delicate juncture. If her pride was fighting an inner battle with good sense, the safest place for him was on the sidelines.

"Euros," she said at last, "and you'll donate another twenty to the charity of my choice."

Relief all but swamped him, but he kept his tone casual. "Done. But I want input on the charity. Kids or animals, or we can split it between them."

"Fine." No handshake, but her tone was all business. "Two weeks isn't much time so don't expect to fart around. Be here tomorrow at ten sharp. I'll give you a few minutes to describe your exaggerated expectations, I'll whittle them down to reality, and then we'll get started."

He cocked an eyebrow. Was that how she saw this relationship? She gave the orders; he obeyed without question?

Fat chance. She might be the expert, but if she thought that also made her the boss, she had another think coming. The upper hand was *always* the same hand holding the checkbook. Namely his.

He'd be sure to enlighten her on that point, but not today, not until after she'd spent a night mentally paying down her bills or sprucing up her studio. After she'd imagined spending the money it would be harder for her to back out, so he'd wait till tomorrow to lay down the law.

In the meantime, though, as he made for the exit he couldn't resist saying over his shoulder, "Ten o'clock is fine. I'll meet you at the café on the corner. Don't be late. I'd hate to dock your pay on day one."

With that, he ducked out the door, narrowly dodging the water bottle that sailed through behind him.

About the Author

Award-winning author **CARA CONNELLY** writes sexy romantic comedies featuring smart sassy women and the hot alpha men who love them. Her internationally bestselling Save the Date series has been described as "emotionally complex," "intensely passionate," and "laugh-out-loud hilarious."

A recovering attorney, Cara recently relocated to Florida with her rock 'n roll husband Billy and their blue-eyed rescue dog Bella. Catch up with her at CaraConnelly.com, sign up for her news, and follow her on Bookbub, Goodreads, Facebook, and Instagram.

Discover great authors, exclusive offers, and more at hc.com.